Thornes Classic Short Stories

D1784400

SHORT STORIES

by

HANS ANDERSEN

TRANSLATED BY ERIK HAUGAARD

EDITED BY SARAH MATTHEWS
AND MIKE ROYSTON

SERIES EDITOR: MIKE ROYSTON

Stanley Thornes (Publishers) Ltd

Support material © Sarah Matthews and Mike Royston 1996

Translation © 1974 Erik Christian Haugaard

Original line illustrations © Stanley Thornes (Publishers) Ltd 1996

The right of Sarah Matthews and Mike Royston to be identified as authors of all support material has been asserted by them in accordance with the Copyright, Designs and Patents Act 1988.

All rights reserved. No part of this publication may be reproduced or transmitted in any form or by any means, electronic or mechanical, including photocopy, recording or any information storage and retrieval system, without permission in writing from the publisher or under licence from the Copyright Licensing Agency Limited. Further details of such licences (for reprographic reproduction) may be obtained from the Copyright Licensing Agency Limited, 90 Tottenham Court Road, London W1P 9HE.

This edition first published in 1996 by:
Stanley Thornes (Publishers) Ltd
Ellenborough House
Wellington Street
CHELTENHAM GL50 1YW
England

96 97 98 99 00 / 10 9 8 7 6 5 4 3 2 1

A catalogue record for this book is available from the British Library.

ISBN 0–7487–2484–2

Acknowledgements

The author and publishers are grateful to the following for permission to reproduce illustrations and photographs:
Hans Andersen Museum, Odense, pages 2, 5
Mansell Collection, pages 3, 4, 6
Mary Evans Picture Library, pages 7, 8

Typeset by DP Press, Kent
Illustrated by Beverly Curl
Printed and bound in Great Britain at T J Press (Padstow) Ltd, Cornwall

Contents

How to use this book

This book contains four short stories by Hans Andersen. It is designed so that you can read the stories on your own, or share your reading with others. Whichever way you read, the stories have been chosen above all to be *enjoyed*.

The Introduction contains:

- a brief account of the writer's life. This gives you an impression of the kind of person he was and outlines the most important things that happened to him during his lifetime.

- a background to the stories, in words and pictures. This explains how the stories came to be written, as well as pointing out some of the main themes and ideas running through them.

To help you get the most from them, the stories have been presented in a particular way. They contain the following features:

- boxes at the beginning of each story, and at other key points, which suggest what you should look out for as you read.

- a glossary at the foot of every page giving the meanings of words you may find unfamiliar.

- a commentary summarising what is happening on each page of the story, to help you follow it as you read.

During each story, you will now and again come across a 'Pause for Playback' section. This contains brief questions to highlight important points in the part of the story you have just read. You can make up your own mind about the 'answers'. They do not have to be written down.

After each story, there is a Study guide. This contains activities designed to help you form an understanding of the story as a whole. Some activities are for small groups, some are for pairs, and some for doing by yourself.

At the end of the book, you will find an Overview section. This asks you to think further about how the stories are written and to make some comparisons between them.

Enjoy your reading!

Introduction

ABOUT THE WRITER

When he was 50 years old, Hans Andersen published his autobiography, *The Fairy Tale of My Life*. But he did not set out to be a writer of fairy tales, nor did his life have a fairy-tale beginning.

Hans Christian Andersen was born on 2 April 1805, in the small Danish town of Odense. His father was a shoemaker, as his own father had been before him. Hans's mother, though a caring and religious woman herself, came from a less respectable background. *Her* mother had not been married to her father. Nor had she been married to the different fathers of her other two daughters, Hans's aunts.

Hans Andersen, then, was brought up as the only son of two strangely matched parents. His father was practical, intelligent and widely read; his mother was steeped in local superstitions, a believer in witchcraft and magic spells. Yet both parents doted on their young son. Hans's father spent almost all his spare time playing with him, making toy theatres and paper cut-outs, reading him stories and plays, and sharing with him the rich stock of folk tales that he loved.

The house in Odense, where Hans Andersen grew up. This picture was drawn in 1836.

When Hans was 11, his father died. He had never made much money from shoe-making. Now the family was poorer than ever, and Hans's mother was forced to work as a washerwoman to make ends meet. Two years later, she re-married. Her second husband was also a shoemaker, but a more successful one. The family was able to move to a bigger house in Odense, though they were never well-off.

By now, Hans was nearing the age when he would have to make his own living. His one wish was to be an actor. In 1819, aged 14, he set out for Copenhagen – the capital of Denmark – to seek his fortune on the stage. He had little money and few patrons who might help him succeed.

Copenhagen, the capital of Denmark, in about 1820

In fact, Hans had neither the looks nor the talent for acting. He spent the next few years miserably poor, frustrated and depressed. He found no regular work. Eventually, it was agreed that he must get a decent education if he were to have any sort of career. A group of friends chipped in to pay his way through school. At the age of 17, six years older than the other students in his class, Hans started Grammar School.

Jenny Lind

It was not a happy time for him. He lived in the house of his headmaster, an ill-tempered and unpleasant man. Hans found schoolwork both difficult and boring. He was a tall, gangling and sensitive boy, given to violent swings of mood. However, he finally won through, and in 1828, at the age of 23, he passed his entrance exam for Copenhagen University.

In the same year, Hans had one of his plays staged, and published a book of humorous writings, *A Walking Tour*. In 1829 he brought out a collection of poems. At last he was gaining recognition and, more important, making some money. His career as a writer had begun.

From 1830 onwards, Hans Andersen turned to full-time writing. He published poems, plays and short stories. Then, in 1835, he produced the first four of the *Fairy Tales* that were to make him famous. By the time he died at the age of 70, he had written over one hundred and fifty of these. He had become known throughout Europe and was on familiar terms with dukes, kings and princes.

His personal life, however, was less happy. He fell in love a number of times, but never married. Perhaps his greatest love was the famous Swedish singer, Jenny Lind, who cared deeply for him as a friend but who never returned his romantic feelings. She was known as 'The Swedish Nightingale'. The fourth story in this volume was written partly as a tribute to her.

In the end, it was through his *Fairy Stories and Tales* that Hans Andersen created happiness for himself, as well as for generations of his readers. It is not hard to see why he called these stories – with their magical events, their lively characters, and their happy endings – 'my gift to the world'.

Hans Christian Andersen

BACKGROUND TO THE STORIES

H ans Andersen is always thought of as Denmark's greatest writer. Yet for most of his life he struggled to have his work valued in his own country.

Story booklets

None of Andersen's 156 fairy tales and stories was first published in book form. In Denmark between 1835 and 1870, stories were almost always printed as small-sized booklets. They had no illustrations and were not bound. They were sold as cheaply as comics are today.

If they proved popular with readers, these booklets – which normally contained between three and eight stories – were collected and published as hard-back books. Only in 1874, a year before his death, did Andersen get the chance to bring out a full Danish edition of his *Fairy Tales and Stories*.

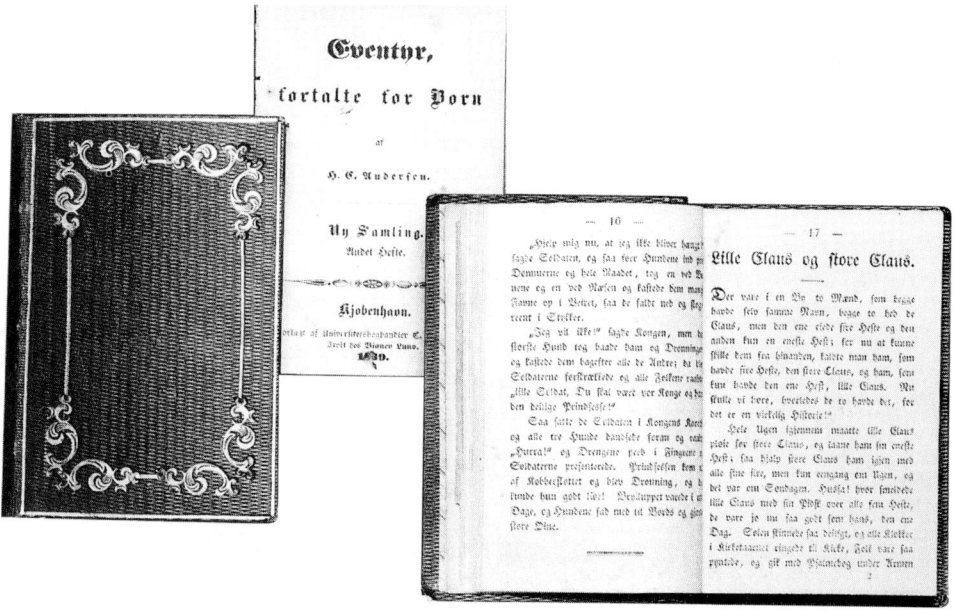

Two pages, the title page and the cover from an early edition of Andersen's Fairy Tales and Stories, *published in 1835*

Overseas publications

Andersen always wrote in his native language. However, a large number of his stories were first published abroad, especially in Germany and England, and later in America. Andersen personally supervised the translation of his work into German, but not into English. The first complete translation of the *Fairy Tales and Stories* only appeared in Britain as recently as 1972.

Who are they for?

Given their publishing history, it is not surprising that there are many different versions of Hans Andersen's stories. They vary widely, often wildly. Some of the best-known have been adapted for very young children, and bear little resemblance to what Andersen really wrote. So, by whom did the author *himself* intend his *Fairy Tales and Stories* to be read?

'A writer for all ages'

Near the end of his life, Andersen was told of a statue being planned in his honour. It would show him surrounded by a crowd of children, all waiting eagerly to have another story read to them. Far from being flattered by the idea, Andersen was furious. 'My blood boiled,' he wrote. 'My aim was to be a writer for *all* ages.'

There is no doubt, then, that Hans Andersen meant his *Fairy Tales* for readers of any and every age-group, including adults. You may know the more appropriate statue that now stands looking out from Copenhagen harbour, offering Andersen's 'gift to the world' (that is, his stories) to all who are able to read them with imagination and understanding.

Cartoon and film forms

In our own day and age, there have been countless film animations and cartoon versions of tales such as *The Ugly Duckling* and *The Little Match Girl*. Good as they often are, these have kept alive the myth that Andersen is a writer only of 'kids' stuff'. In fact, nothing could be further from the truth. Read *The Snow Queen* in this volume and see what *you* think.

As for those cartoon versions…Have you seen the animated films of *Superman* and *Animal Farm* or any of Shakespeare's plays? It is the way we *respond* to them, rather than the stories in themselves, which dictates 'who they are for'.

The statue of The Little Mermaid, in the harbour at Copenhagen

Fairy tales

We all tell stories all the time. Through them, we interest and amuse people by picturing in words 'what happened when...' – in the Maths lesson, at the disco, during the football match. Through them, too, we try to make *sense* of the world we live in, where things often happen in a jumbled, unexpected, seemingly senseless way. Writers of fairy tales do exactly the same.

Magic stories

Before writing was invented, stories were being told and passed on by word of mouth. They were also drawn and painted. Cave paintings, for example, told stories of what had happened on a hunt – and of what the hunters *hoped* would happen next time. Such stories were partly magic. By showing pictures of animals being speared, cave painters hoped to make real animals come close enough to be killed. Their paintings were a way of controlling the wild world. So, very often, are stories.

An ancient cave painting

Ordering our lives

Fairy tales give the world an *order* we would like it to have. In real life, being very good and very clever does not guarantee that you won't be killed. But in the world of fairy tales we know that Little Red Riding Hood *will* survive, and that the Wolf is bound to die. Once Aladdin has got the right combination of words, the cave door will open. In fairy tales magic spells always work. Being good brings rewards: being bad brings punishments. The world of fairy tales is one of certainties. Nobody has any real doubts, nobody changes (except on a temporary basis), and everybody gets what's coming to them.

Fables

Hans Andersen did more than any other writer to make popular the fictional world of fairy tales, with its magic certainties and happy endings. His stories are also linked closely to the much older tradition of fable.

In fables, human weaknesses are pointed out – often through animal characters – and the right way of behaving is summed up in a neat moral, or lesson, at the end. Think of any fables you know by the ancient Greek writer Aesop: *The Tortoise and the Hare*, for instance. In the eighteenth-century fable of *The Fox and the Crow*, the fox flatters the crow so effectively about its beautiful singing voice that the vain and silly bird drops the cheese it has stolen. The fox gets the cheese. The moral: pride goes before a fall (or eat up your cheese before singing to foxes!).

An illustration to the fable of The Tortoise and the Hare

'Once upon a time...?'

If, in fairy tales, 'anything can happen', it can also happen anywhere at any time. Hans Andersen's stories are not bound by time or place. They are about things that happen *all* the time, and which are likely to keep on happening. In many stories and films of today, magical powers, human weakness and moral goodness are all important elements – just as they are in *The Tinderbox* and *The Emperor's New Clothes*. In its own way, *Superman* is a fairy tale, isn't it?

OTHER RECOMMENDED STORIES BY HANS ANDERSEN

Inchelina

The Magic Galoshes

The Wild Swans

Mother Elderberry

The Red Shoes

The Old House

Everything In Its Right Place

The Millennium

She Was No Good

Clod Hans

The Bog King's Daughter

The Bell Deep

Anne Lisbeth

A String Of Pearls

What Father Does Is Always Right

The Ice Maiden

In The Children's Room

The Rags

The Year's Story

The Cripple

You can find these stories in *Hans Andersen: The Complete Fairy Tales and Stories* translated by Erik Christian Haugaard (Victor Gollancz, 1974).

THE EMPEROR'S NEW CLOTHES

Look out for...
- **how the two swindlers make themselves a lot of money.**
- **why all the adults in the story fall for the swindlers' tricks.**
- **the little child – why is he not fooled in the same way everyone else is?**

Many, many years ago there was an emperor who was so terribly fond of beautiful new clothes that he spent all his money on his attire. He did not care about his soldiers, or attending the theatre, or even going for a drive in the park, unless it was to show off his new clothes. He had an outfit for every hour of the day. And just as we say, 'The king is in his council chamber,' his subjects used to say, 'The emperor is in his clothes closet.'

In the large town where the emperor's palace was, life was gay and happy; and every day new visitors arrived. One day two swindlers came. They told everybody that they were weavers and that they could weave the most marvellous cloth. Not only were the colours and the patterns of their material extraordinarily beautiful, but the cloth had the strange quality of being invisible to anyone who was unfit for his office or unforgivably stupid.

'This is truly marvellous,' thought the emperor. 'Now if I had robes cut from that material, I should know which of my councillors was unfit for his office, and I would be able to pick out my clever subjects myself. They must

---

COMMENTARY

Two 'con men' arrive in the emperor's city. They have heard he is extremely vain about his appearance. They plan to cheat him by saying that they can weave a special kind of cloth with magic powers.

attire: clothing
swindlers: cheats, confidence tricksters
unfit for his office: not able to do his job properly
councillors: advisers

weave some material for me!' And he gave the swindlers a lot of money so they
could start working at once.

They set up a loom and acted as if they were weaving, but the loom was
empty. The fine silk and gold threads they demanded from the emperor they
never used, but hid them in their own knapsacks. Late into the night they
would sit before their empty loom, pretending to weave.

'I would like to know how they are getting along,' thought the emperor;
but his heart beat strangely when he remembered that those who were
stupid or unfit for their office would not be able to see the material. Not
that he was really worried that this would happen to him. Still, it might be
better to send someone else the first time and see how he fared.
Everybody in town had heard about the cloth's magic quality and most of
them could hardly wait to find out how stupid or unworthy their
neighbours were.

'I shall send my faithful prime minister over to see how the weavers are
getting along,' thought the emperor. 'He will know how to judge the material,
for he is both clever and fit for his office, if any man is.'

The good-natured old man stepped into the room where the weavers were
working and saw the empty loom. He closed his eyes, and opened them again.
'God preserve me!' he thought. 'I cannot see a thing!' But he didn't say it
out loud.

The swindlers asked him to step a little closer to the loom so that he could
admire the intricate patterns and marvellous colours of the material they were
weaving. They both pointed to the empty loom, and the poor old prime
minister opened his eyes as wide as he could; but it didn't help, he still
couldn't see anything.

'Am I stupid?' he thought. 'I can't believe it, but if so, it is best no one finds
out about it. But maybe I am not fit for my office. No, that is worse, I'd better
not admit that I can't see what they are weaving.'

'Tell us what you think of it,' demanded one of the swindlers.

'It is beautiful. It is very lovely,' mumbled the old prime minister, adjusting

knapsacks: strong leather or canvas bags,
   worn strapped to the back
fared: got on
intricate: complicated

COMMENTARY
The emperor sets the 'weavers' to
work. They steal the silk and gold he
gives them, and carry on pretending to
make their magic cloth.
   In time, the emperor sends his
prime minister to find out how the
work is going. The old man cannot see
anything, but he dare not say so.

his glasses. 'What patterns! What colours! I shall tell the emperor that it pleases me ever so much.'

'That is a compliment,' both the weavers said; and now they described the patterns and told which shades of colour they had used. The prime minister listened attentively, so that he could repeat their words to the emperor; and that is exactly what he did.

The two swindlers demanded more money, and more silk and gold thread. They said they had to use it for their weaving, but their loom remained as empty as ever.

Soon the emperor sent another of his trusted councillors to see how the work was progressing. He looked and looked just as the prime minister had, but since there was nothing to be seen, he didn't see anything.

'Isn't it a marvellous piece of material?' asked one of the swindlers; and they both began to describe the beauty of their cloth again.

'I am not stupid,' thought the emperor's councillor. 'I must be unfit for my office. That is strange; but I'd better not admit it to anyone.' And he started to praise the material, which he could not see, for the loveliness of its patterns and colours.

'I think it is the most charming piece of material I have ever seen,' declared the councillor to the emperor.

Everyone in town was talking about the marvellous cloth that the swindlers were weaving.

PAUSE FOR PLAYBACK:
Now look at the playback questions on page 17 before going on with your reading.

At last the emperor himself decided to see it before it was removed from the loom. Attended by the most important people in the empire, among them the prime minister and the councillor who had been there before, the emperor

COMMENTARY
The prime minister doesn't want to look stupid or unfit for his job. He reports back to the emperor that the cloth is amazingly beautiful.

After a while, the emperor sends another courtier to check on the weavers' work. Not wanting to seem foolish, he too says that the cloth is 'marvellous'.

attentively: with careful concentration

entered the room where the weavers were weaving furiously on their empty loom.

'Isn't it *magnifique*?' asked the prime minister.

'Your Majesty, look at the colours and the patterns,' said the councillor.

And the two old gentlemen pointed to the empty loom, believing that all the rest of the company could see the cloth.

'What!' thought the emperor. 'I can't see a thing!' Why, this is a disaster! Am I stupid? Am I unfit to be emperor! Oh, it is too horrible!' Aloud he said, 'It is very lovely. It has my approval,' while he nodded his head and looked at the empty loom.

All the councillors, ministers, and men of great importance who had come with him stared and stared; but they saw no more than the emperor had seen, and they said the same thing that he had said, 'It is lovely.' And they advised him to have clothes cut and sewn, so that he could wear them in the procession at the next great celebration.

'It is magnificent! Beautiful! Excellent!' All of their mouths agreed, though none of their eyes had seen anything. The two swindlers were decorated and given the title 'Royal Knight of the Loom.'

The night before the procession, the two swindlers didn't sleep at all. They had sixteen candles lighting up the room where they worked. Everyone could see how busy they were, getting the emperor's new clothes finished. They pretended to take the cloth from the loom; they cut the air with their big scissors, and sewed with needles without thread. At last they announced: 'The emperor's clothes are ready!'

Together with his courtiers, the emperor came. The swindlers lifted their arms as if they were holding something in their hands, and said, 'These are the trousers. This is the robe, and here is the train. They are all as light as if they were made of spider webs! It will be as if Your Majesty had almost nothing on, but that is their special virtue.'

'Oh yes,' breathed all the courtiers; but they saw nothing, for there was nothing to be seen.

---

magnifique: French for 'magnificent'
courtiers: the emperor's servants and
  advisers

COMMENTARY

The emperor decides to see the magic cloth for himself. Just like his courtiers, he can see nothing. But just like them, he says it is quite beautiful so as not to seem stupid. He orders the cloth to be made into robes for him to wear at a state procession.

At last the swindlers announce that the clothes are ready.

'Will Your Imperial Majesty be so gracious as to take off your clothes?' asked the swindlers. 'Over there by the big mirror, we shall help you put your new ones on.'

The emperor did as he was told; and the swindlers acted as if they were dressing him in the clothes they should have made. Finally they tied around his waist the long train which two of his most noble courtiers were to carry.

The emperor stood in front of the mirror admiring the clothes he couldn't see.

'Oh, how they suit you! A perfect fit!' everyone exclaimed. 'What colours! What patterns! The new clothes are magnificent!'

'The crimson canopy, under which Your Imperial Majesty is to walk, is waiting outside,' said the imperial master of court ceremony.

'Well, I am dressed. Aren't my clothes becoming?' The emperor turned around once more in front of the mirror, pretending to study his finery.

The two gentlemen of the imperial bedchamber fumbled on the floor, trying to find the train which they were supposed to carry. They didn't dare admit that they didn't see anything, so they pretended to pick up the train and held their hands as if they were carrying it.

The emperor walked in the procession under his crimson canopy. And all the people of the town, who had lined the streets or were looking down from the windows, said the emperor's clothes were beautiful. 'What a magnificent robe! And the train! How well the emperor's clothes suit him!'

None of them were willing to admit that they hadn't seen a thing; for if anyone did, then he was either stupid or unfit for the job he held. Never before had the emperor's clothes been such a success.

'But he doesn't have anything on!' cried a little child.

'Listen to the innocent one,' said the proud father. And the people whispered among each other and repeated what the child had said.

'He doesn't have anything on. There's a little child who says that he has nothing on.'

'He has nothing on!' shouted all the people at last.

COMMENTARY

The emperor, still sure that everyone else can see the clothes but himself, pretends to put them on. He sets off with his courtiers to take part in the procession.

The townspeople cheer the emperor's magic clothes. They are convinced that only *they* can't see them.

Then a small child says loudly that the emperor is wearing nothing at all.

the long train: a long, sweeping cloak
canopy: a square sunshade with poles at each corner
becoming: handsome

The emperor shivered, for he was certain that they were right; but he thought, 'I must bear it until the procession is over.' And he walked even more proudly, and the two gentlemen of the imperial bedchamber went on carrying the train that wasn't there.

PAUSE FOR PLAYBACK:
Now look at the playback questions on page 17,

COMMENTARY
Everyone realises that their emperor has been tricked. He walks on, naked — feeling very foolish inside.

Study guide

PAGES 11 to 13:

- ➤ Up to now, what do you think of the emperor? How would you describe his character?
- ➤ Why do you think the swindlers' 'con trick' is being so successful?
- ➤ Do you feel that the emperor's courtiers are bad people?
- ➤ How do you predict the story might end? Will the swindlers get away with it – or will they be found out?

Now return to reading the story on page 13

PAGES 13 to 16:

- ➤ Why do the courtiers agree with the emperor that the cloth is *'magnifique'*?
- ➤ Why do you think the townspeople say that the emperor's clothes are beautiful? Would *you*, if you were in the crowd?
- ➤ The writer makes a small child, rather than an adult, come out with the truth. Why do you think he chooses to do this?
- ➤ If you were the emperor at the end of the story, what would your feelings be? What might you do after the procession was over?

REVIEWING THE WHOLE STORY: SUGGESTED ACTIVITIES

1 The Great Swindle

a   **With a partner**, imagine that you are the two swindlers in the story. Before you go to the emperor's city, you send his prime minister (i) a poster and (ii) a letter advertising your services.

First, re-read all the passages in which the behaviour of the swindlers is described. Look closely at how they play on the *vanity* of the emperor and his courtiers.

Now plan and design your poster (or 'flyer') using a single sheet of plain paper.

Re-read the start of the story to remind yourselves of (i) who you are pretending to be, and (ii) what you are claiming to be able to do. Then:

● make up a name for your 'firm';

● design a suitable logo;

● word the poster, saying briefly what you have to offer;

● list the prices you charge.

Produce the finished version of your poster. Use different kinds of lettering and illustrate it in colour as attractively as possible. It can form part of a class display.

b   **By yourself**, write the advertising letter you will send to the prime minister. If you wish, type or word-process it.

The letter should say in more detail than the poster:

● what wonderful things you are able to do for the emperor;

● what experience you have had working for other clients;

● why your firm is the best in the business.

Include anything else you think will help 'sell' your services.

Write in a suitably formal style, using Standard English. You need to lay out the letter properly – make up an impressive address for the emperor's palace – and end it 'Yours faithfully'. Then sign off, using interesting names for yourselves.

2 | Picturing the story

By yourself, draw a cartoon version of *The Emperor's New Clothes*. You need not be a talented artist: stick figures will do.

On a sheet of rough paper, plan about *ten* cartoon frames to make sure you tell the story in order, and in full.

Underneath each frame write *two* different kinds of caption:

● the first caption will describe, in your own words, what's happening in the story at this particular point;

● the second caption will describe the *thoughts* of each character shown in the frame.

This is an example of what your first frame might look like:

The emperor enjoyed nothing more than trying on a new suit of clothes.

Emperor: *How incredibly handsome I look! What a sensation I'll make in the state procession.*

Servant: *How much longer is the fat fool going to stand in front of this mirror? He's completely gross!*

Your finished cartoon version of the story can form part of a class display. It will look more attractive if you colour it in and/or use computer graphics.

3 | A front-page news report for *The Emperor's Own Paper*

After the procession described at the end of the story, *The Daily Scandal* wrote an account of it that began like this:

Emperor shows what he's made of in Nude Walkabout

Has he lost his marbles as well as his clothes?

The report contained embarrassing photographs and a long interview with the child who said 'He's got nothing on!'

Before this report could be printed, the prime minister found out about it. The emperor had the editor of *The Daily Scandal* shot. The photographers were imprisoned for life, and the child mysteriously disappeared from home.

You are employed as a court journalist on *The Emperor's Own Paper*. You have been commanded to write a 'correct' report of the procession, using this headline:

Emperor Magnificent in new robes for State Procession

Royal weavers to receive knighthoods

Plan, draft and write your front-page report.

How to work

a   **As a class**, look at some front-page stories from your local newspaper. Talk about:

- the content and layout of the *first* paragraph of the story;

- how the rest of the story is built up through a series of short paragraphs;

- the way in which interviews are worked into the story;

- the purpose of illustrations and the captions below them;

- the style in which the story is written;

- how subtitles are used to help the reader.

b   **With a partner**, decide how you are going to write *your* front page. Remember that all the way through you have to pretend the procession was a 'triumphal' success which the emperor and everyone else enjoyed.

Discuss together what to describe, and how to describe it, so as to bring out the special atmosphere of this royal occasion.

c   **With your partner**, plan who is going to be interviewed and what they will say. Most front-page stories include *several* interviews.

Now decide how to set out the whole front page. You will need to think about illustrations and captions. How much space are these going to take up?

d   **By yourself**, write a draft of the whole newspaper report. Show it to your teacher for comment. Do a thorough check for any mistakes of spelling, punctuation and grammar.

Then produce your front page in its final form. It should look as much like 'the real thing' as possible. Choose the size of paper you want to use. If you wish, do it on a computer.

4   Playscript: a royal show-down with the swindlers

After the state procession, imagine that the emperor calls the two swindlers to his palace. He wants to tell them what he thinks of them before sending them on their way. The prime minister is also present.

a   **In a group**, talk about and plan this conversation as if it were a scene from a play. Bear in mind that:

● the emperor will be feeling a mixture of emotions – anger, embarrassment, shame, etc. – but that, above all, he will want to remain *dignified*.

● the swindlers are very cunning and will try to talk their way out of trouble.

b   Working together, write a script of the conversation that takes place. The characters will speak to each other in a *formal* way – emperors do not go in for abuse.

c   When you are happy with your script, act it out to the rest of the class or on to tape.

THE TINDERBOX

Look out for...
- **the way in which the soldier behaves. What kind of person is he? Does he change as the story goes on?**
- **what happens to the witch, and to the king and queen. Is it fair that they end up as they do?**

A soldier came marching down the road: Left...right! Left...right! He had a pack on his back and a sword at his side. He had been in the war and he was on his way home. Along the road he met a witch. She was a disgusting sight, with a lower lip that hung all the way down to her chest.

'Good evening, young soldier,' she said. 'What a handsome sword you have and what a big knapsack. I can see that you are a real soldier! I shall give you all the money that you want.'

'Thank you, old witch,' he said.

'Do you see that big tree?' asked the witch, and pointed to the one they were standing next to. 'The trunk is hollow. You climb up to the top of the tree, crawl into the hole, and slide deep down inside it. I'll tie a rope around your waist, so I can pull you up again when you call me.'

'What am I supposed to do down in the tree?' asked the soldier.

'Get money!' answered the witch and laughed. 'Now listen to me. When you get down to the very bottom, you'll be in a great passageway where you'll be able to see because there are over a hundred lamps burning. You'll find

COMMENTARY
A soldier returning from the war meets a witch. She offers him all the money he could possibly want if only he will climb down inside a hollow tree.

knapsack: see page 12 for an explanation

three doors; and you can open them all because the keys are in the locks. Go into the first one; and there on a chest, in the middle of the room, you'll see a dog with eyes as big as teacups. Don't let that worry you. You will have my blue checked apron; just spread it out on the floor, put the dog down on top of it, and it won't do you any harm. Open the chest and take as many coins as you wish, they are all copper. If it's silver you're after, then go into the next room. There you'll find a dog with eyes as big as millstones; but don't let that worry you, put him on the apron and take the money. If you'd rather have gold, you can have that too; it's in the third room. Wait till you see that dog, he's got eyes as big as the Round Tower in Copenhagen; but don't let that worry you. Put him down on my apron and he won't hurt you; then you can take as much gold as you wish.'

'That doesn't sound bad!' said the soldier. 'But what am I to do for you, old witch? I can't help thinking that you must want something too.'

'No,' replied the witch. 'I don't want one single coin. Just bring me the old tinderbox that my grandmother forgot the last time she was down there.'

'I'm ready, tie the rope around my waist!' ordered the soldier.

'There you are, and here is my blue checked apron,' said the witch.

The soldier climbed the tree, let himself fall into the hole, and found that he was in the passageway, where more than a hundred lights burned.

He opened the first door. Oh! There sat the dog with eyes as big as teacups glaring at him.

'You are a handsome fellow!' he exclaimed as he put the dog down on the witch's apron. He filled his pockets with copper coins, closed the chest, and put the dog back on top of it.

He went into the second room. Aha! There sat the dog with eyes as big as millstones. 'Don't keep looking at me like that,' said the soldier good-naturedly. 'It isn't polite and you'll spoil your eyes.' He put the dog down on the witch's apron and opened the chest. When he saw all the silver coins, he emptied the copper out of his pockets and filled both them and his knapsack with silver.

millstones: large round stones used to grind flour in a mill

tinderbox: before matches were invented, people used a box containing dry scraps of linen. These would catch alight from sparks made by striking steel against a flint

COMMENTARY

The witch explains what the soldier needs to do. She wants him to bring up from the tree an old tinderbox of her grandmother's, and give it to her.

The soldier climbs down into the tree. At the bottom he meets three dogs. Each has eyes bigger than the last.

Now he entered the third room. That dog was big enough to frighten anyone, even a soldier. His eyes were as large as the Round Tower in Copenhagen and they turned around like wheels.

'Good evening,' said the soldier politely, taking off his cap, for such a dog he had never seen before. For a while he just stood looking at it; but finally he said to himself, 'Enough of this!' Then he put the dog down on the witch's apron and opened the chest.

'God preserve me!' he cried. There was so much gold that there was enough to buy the whole city of Copenhagen; and all the ginger-bread men, rocking horses, riding whips, and tin soldiers in the whole world.

Quickly the soldier threw away all the silver coins that he had in his pockets and knapsack and put gold in them instead; he even filled his boots and his cap with money. He put the dog back on the chest, closed the door behind him, and called up through the hollow tree.

'Pull me up, you old witch!'

'Have you got the tinderbox?' she called back.

'Right you are, I have forgotten it,' he replied honestly, and went back to get it. The witch hoisted him up and again he stood on the road; but now his pockets, knapsack, cap, and boots were filled with gold and he felt quite differently.

'Why do you want the tinderbox?' he asked.

'Mind your own business,' answered the witch crossly. 'You have got your money, just give me the tinderbox.'

'Blah! Blah!' said the soldier. 'Tell me what you are going to use it for, right now; or I'll draw my sword and cut off your head.'

'No!' replied the witch firmly; but that was a mistake, for the soldier chopped her head off. She lay there dead. The soldier put all his gold in her apron, tied it up in a bundle, and threw it over his shoulder. The tinderbox he dropped into his pocket; and off to town he went.

The town was nice, and the soldier went to the nicest inn, where he asked to be put up in the finest room and ordered all the things he liked to eat best

COMMENTARY

The soldier collects copper, silver and gold coins from the treasure chests guarded by the dogs. In his excitement, the soldier forgets the tinderbox – but the witch reminds him and he goes back for it. She then hauls him back up to ground level.

By now, the soldier suspects the witch is up to something. He asks her why she wants the tinderbox. She refuses to tell him, so he kills her.

He sets off to town with his pockets full of gold.

for his supper, because now he had so much money that he was rich.

The servant who polished his boots thought it was very odd that a man so wealthy should have such worn-out boots. But the soldier hadn't had time to buy anything yet; the next day he bought boots and clothes that fitted his purse. And the soldier became a refined gentlemen. People were eager to tell him all about their town and their king, and what a lovely princess his daughter was.

'I would like to see her,' said the soldier.

'But no one sees her,' explained the townsfolk. 'She lives in a copper castle, surrounded by walls, and towers, and a moat. The king doesn't dare allow anyone to visit her because it has been foretold that she will marry a simple soldier, and the king doesn't want that to happen.'

PAUSE FOR PLAYBACK:
Now look at the playback questions on page 31 before going on with your reading.

'If only I could see her,' thought the soldier, though it was unthinkable.

The soldier lived merrily, went to the theatre, kept a carriage so he could drive in the king's park, and gave lots of money to the poor. He remembered well what it felt like not to have a penny in his purse.

He was rich and well dressed. He had many friends; and they all said that he was kind and a real cavalier; and such things he liked to hear. But since he used money every day and never received any, he soon had only two copper coins left.

He had to move out of the beautiful room downstairs, up to a tiny one in the garret, where he not only polished his boots himself but also mended them with a large needle. None of his friends came to see him, for they said there were too many stairs to climb.

It was a very dark evening and he could not even buy a candle. Suddenly

---

fitted his purse: showed how rich he was
foretold: prophesied, already known
unthinkable: out of the question
cavalier: a rich nobleman
garret: attic

COMMENTARY
In the town the soldier lives a life of luxury. Soon he hears about the king's beautiful daughter who lives locked in a tower. He longs to meet her.

Before long, the soldier spends all his money. He is forced to live in an old attic. None of his friends come to visit him.

he remembered that he had seen the stub of a candle in the tinderbox that he had brought up from the bottom of the hollow tree. He found the tinderbox and took out the candle. He struck the flint. There was a spark, and in through the door came the dog with eyes as big as teacups.

'What does my master command?' asked the dog.

'What's this all about?' exclaimed the soldier. 'That certainly was an interesting tinderbox. Can I have whatever I want? Bring some money,' he ordered. In less time than it takes to say thank you, the dog was gone and back with a big sack of copper coins in his mouth.

Now the soldier understood why the witch had thought the tinderbox so valuable. If he struck it once, the dog appeared who sat on the chest full of copper coins; if he struck it twice, then the dog came who guarded the silver money; and if he struck it three times, then came the one who had the gold.

The soldier moved downstairs again, wore fine clothes again, and had fine friends, for now they all remembered him and cared for him as they had before.

One night, when he was sitting alone after his friends had gone, he thought, 'It is a pity that no one can see that beautiful princess. What is the good of her beauty if she must always remain behind the high walls and towers of a copper castle? Will I never see her?…Where is my tinderbox?'

He made the sparks fly and the dog with eyes as big as teacups came. 'I know it's very late at night,' he said, 'but I would so like to see the beautiful princess, if only for a minute.'

Away went the dog; and faster than thought he returned with the sleeping princess on his back. She was so lovely that anyone would have known that she was a real princess. The soldier could not help kissing her, for he was a true soldier.

The dog brought the princess back to her copper castle; but in the morning while she was having tea with her father and mother, the king and queen, she told them that she had had a very strange dream that night. A large dog had come and carried her away to a soldier who kissed her.

COMMENTARY

One day, feeling cold, the soldier tries to light a fire by using the tinderbox. He finds that it has magic powers: whenever he strikes it, one of the huge-eyed dogs appears and does whatever he asks it to. The soldier becomes rich again.

One night, he commands one of the dogs to fetch the princess to him. It does so. He kisses the sleeping princess, then sends her back to the royal castle.

'That's a nice story,' said the queen, but she didn't mean it.

The next night one of the older ladies in waiting was sent to watch over the princess while she slept, and find out whether it had only been a dream, and not something worse.

The soldier longed to see the princess so much that he couldn't bear it, so at night he sent the dog to fetch her. The dog ran as fast as he could, but the lady in waiting had her boots on and she kept up with him all the way. When she saw which house he had entered, she took out a piece of chalk and made a big white cross on the door.

'Now we'll be able to find it in the morning,' she thought, and went home to get some sleep.

When the dog returned the princess to the castle, he noticed the cross on the door of the house where his master lived; so he took a piece of white chalk and put crosses on all the doors of all the houses in the whole town. It was a very clever thing to do, for now the lady in waiting would never know which was the right door.

The next morning the king and queen, the old lady in waiting, and all the royal officers went out into town to find the house where the princess had been.

'Here it is!' exclaimed the king, when he saw the first door with a cross on it.

'No, my sweet husband, it is here,' said his wife, who had seen the second door with a cross on it.

'Here's one!'

'There's one!'

Everyone shouted at once, for it didn't matter where anyone looked: there he would find a door with a cross on it; and so they all gave up.

Now the queen was so clever, she could do more than ride in a golden carriage. She took out her golden scissors and cut out a large piece of silk and sewed it into a pretty bag. This she filled with the fine grain of buckwheat, and tied the bag around the princess' waist. When this was done, she cut a little hole in the bag just big enough for the little grains of buckwheat to fall

---

lady in waiting: the princess's chief maid
fine grain of buckwheat: small particles of
    corn

COMMENTARY
The queen grows suspicious when she hears her daughter has 'dreamed' of kissing a common soldier. She takes steps to keep her under strict observation the following night.
At first, the queen's plan to find out where the princess goes at night fails.

out, one at a time, and show the way to the house where the princess was taken by the dog.

During the night the dog came to fetch the princess and carry her on his back to the soldier, who loved her so much that now he had only one desire, and that was to be a prince so that he could marry her.

The dog neither saw nor felt the grains of buckwheat that made a little trail all the way from the copper castle to the soldier's room at the inn. In the morning the king and queen had no difficulty in finding where the princess had been, and the soldier was thrown into jail.

There he sat in the dark with nothing to do; and what made matters worse was that everyone said, 'Tomorrow you are going to be hanged!'

That was not amusing to hear. If only he had had his tinderbox, but he had forgotten it in his room. When the sun rose, he watched the people through the bars of his window as they hurried toward the gates of the city, for the hanging was to take place outside the walls. He heard the drums and the royal soldiers marching. Everyone was running. He saw a shoemaker's apprentice, who had not bothered to take off his leather apron and was wearing slippers. The boy lifted his legs so high, it looked as though he were galloping. One of his slippers flew off and landed near the window of the soldier's cell.

'Hey!' shouted the soldier. 'Listen shoemaker, wait a minute, nothing much will happen before I get there. But if you will run to the inn and get the tinderbox I left in my room, you can earn four copper coins. But you'd better use your legs or it will be too late.'

The shoemaker's apprentice, who didn't have one copper coin, was eager to earn four; and he ran to get the tinderbox as fast as he could; and gave it to the soldier.

And now you shall hear what happened after that!

Outside the gates of the town, a gallows had been built; around it stood the royal soldiers and many hundreds of thousands of people. The king and the queen sat on their lovely throne, and opposite them sat the judge and the royal council.

COMMENTARY

The queen is cunning, though. Her second plan works, and she traces the princess to the soldier's house. He is thrown into prison.

The soldier sits sadly in his cell waiting to be hanged. Hearing a young apprentice run past outside, he calls him to fetch the witch's tinderbox.

apprentice: a youngster learning a trade
cell: small room in a prison
gallows: a wooden frame used for hanging people

The soldier was standing on the platform, but as the noose was put around his neck, he declared that it was an ancient custom to grant a condemned man his last innocent wish. They only thing he wanted was to be allowed to smoke a pipe of tobacco.

The king couldn't refuse; and the soldier took out his tinderbox and struck it: once, twice, three times! Instantly, the three dogs were before him: the one with eyes as big as teacups, the one with eyes as big as millstones, and the one with eyes as big as the Round Tower in Copenhagen.

'Help me! I don't want to be hanged!' cried the soldier.

The dogs ran toward the judge and the royal council. They took one man by the leg and another by the nose, and threw them up in the air, so high that when they hit the earth again they broke into little pieces.

'Not me!' screamed the king; but the biggest dog took both the king and queen and sent them flying up as high as all the others had been.

The royal guards got frightened; and the people began to shout: 'Little soldier, you shall be our king and marry the princess!'

The soldier rode in the king's golden carriage; and the three dogs danced in front of it and barked: 'Hurrah!'

The little boys whistled and the royal guards presented arms. The princess came out of her copper castle and became queen, which she liked very much. The wedding feast lasted a week; and the three dogs sat at the table and made eyes at everyone.

PAUSE FOR PLAYBACK:
Now look at the playback questions on page 31.

COMMENTARY
The soldier is taken to be hanged. As he stands with the noose round his neck, he asks if he may have one last pipe of tobacco to smoke.

When the soldier strikes his tinderbox, all three dogs appear. He orders them to rescue him. They kill the king and the queen and all their courtiers. The soldier is now free to marry the princess. After their wedding, they rule the country together. Everyone, including the three dogs, lives happily ever after.

---

noose: the loop of rope put around a   *council:* courtiers
   person's neck to hang them   *made eyes:* looked pleased
condemned: found guilty

Study guide

PLAYBACK QUESTIONS

PAGES 23 TO 26:

- ➤ From what you have read so far, do you think the soldier is brave – as soldiers are meant to be?
- ➤ Is the witch trying to trick the soldier, or does she treat him fairly?
- ➤ Why does the soldier chop off the witch's head? Do you think she deserves to die?
- ➤ The soldier is unknown in the town, yet a lot of people seek his friendship. Why?

Now return to reading the story on page 26

PAGES 26 TO 30:

- ➤ Do you think the soldier is reckless with the money he has suddenly got?
- ➤ Why does the soldier end up in prison? For what reason do you think the king and queen want to see him hanged?
- ➤ If the soldier had not met the witch, whom he killed, would he have escaped death himself?
- ➤ Do you think this story has a moral or 'lesson'? If so, what might it be?

REVIEWING THE WHOLE STORY: SUGGESTED ACTIVITIES

1 An underground map

Recall the first part of the story, where the writer describes the soldier's journey from the base of the tree to the third room in which he finds the chest full of gold.

a **With a partner**, take turns to describe what happens *without looking back at the text*. Include every detail you can remember, however small.

Now take turns to read the passage aloud, dividing it up equally between you. Give yourselves a mark out of ten for how well you remembered it.

b **By yourself**, draw a map or plan of the whole of the soldier's journey underground. Label it clearly, using *quotations* from the story.

Your map might begin like this:

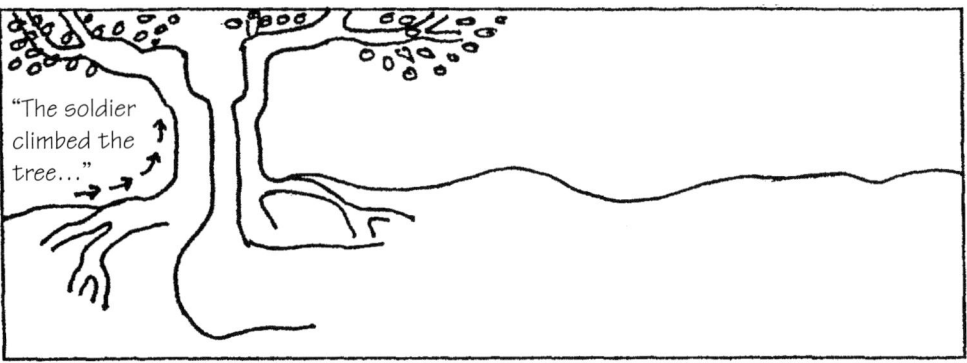

Continue drawing and labelling in this way. Check the text carefully to make sure that all the details are accurate according to the story.

Work on a large sheet of plain paper. Use colour to make your map as clear and accurate as possible.

When you have finished, your map can form part of a class display.

2 Highs and lows: the soldier's story

In the course of the story, the soldier meets with mixed fortunes. For example: sometimes he is happy and successful; sometimes he is extremely miserable; at other times he is in a lot of danger...and so on.

a   **In a group**, skim-read the whole story. Then talk about the 'highs and lows' that the soldier experiences. Find particular points in the text to back up what you say.

In your opinion, when is the soldier (i) at his most happy, (ii) in the most danger, (iii) at his most prosperous, (iv) at his most miserable?

b   **With a partner**, draw a bar graph like the one below to illustrate the highs and lows of the soldier's fortunes.

The bars on your graph will represent *four* things: (i) happiness; (ii) danger; (iii) riches; (iv) misery.

Inside each bar, write a one-sentence summary of what is happening at that particular point in the story.

c   **As a class**, talk about the *causes* of the soldier's changes in fortune. Do you think they result mainly from:

●   his own actions?

●   what other people do?

●   fate?

d   **By yourself**, write a report on what you have done during this activity. Set it out under these headings:

(i)   What we did: the research method.
(ii)   What we found out: the data.
(iii)   How we explained our findings: the theory.

Write in the clear, formal style of a report, using Standard English.

3 | Oh, the agony!

Re-read the passages describing: how and why the princess is locked up (page 26), and her 'dream' (page 27). Imagine that she smuggles out a letter to an 'agony aunt' who writes a column in a teenage magazine. What would she say in it? How would the agony aunt reply?

a **With a partner**, put yourself in the princess's position. Refer back to the story, and use your imagination, to discuss:

● what her life is like in the 'copper castle';

● what she thinks of her parents, the king and queen;

● what she most wants in life;

● the effect on her of her 'dream'.

b **With the same partner**, imagine you are the agony aunt. You have just read the princess's letter and are wondering how best to reply. Talk about the advice you will give her. Will you, for instance, tell her to do what her parents want, or to try kicking up a fuss, or to work out a way of escaping, or…?

c **By yourself**, write *both* letters. In preparation, look at some real agony columns in magazines or newspapers to give you an idea of the style in which they are written. The example below is a light-hearted imitation of the 'real thing' which may help you to begin.

Have you got a problem you can't handle on your own?
Aunty Kitty Advises

Dear Aunty Kitty
Please help me, I don't know what to do. My boyfriend has given me a pet parrot in a cage, but my father has threatened to kill it. The thing is, the parrot makes a lot of noise, and uses a lot of bad language, which my father will not allow in the house. I love my boyfriend very much, and I do not want my father to kill his present to me. What can I do to make the situation better?
Yours despairingly
Bird Lover

Dear Bird Lover
The real question is, how much does your boyfriend love you? Nobody who really cared about you would give you a present that upset your family. Ask him to take the parrot back and keep it at his house. If he loves you he will be happy to do that for you (and it will give you an extra reason for calling round to his house…). Or you can spend your spare time teaching the parrot to stop using bad language, and to say nice things about your father. Don't lose heart, and don't pick up any naughty words!
Aunty Kitty

4 'Get money!'

In *The Tinderbox*, all the main characters – except the princess – are greedy for money.

a **With a partner**, discuss what the following characters do in the story to 'get money':

● the witch.

● the king and queen.

● the soldier.

In particular, talk about (i) the lengths they go to in order to obtain, or to keep their hands on, money (ii) whether or not it makes them happy.

b **Join up with another pair**. Conduct a 'hot seat' interview session, in the following way:

● Three of you take on the roles of the witch, the queen, and the soldier. The fourth member of your group acts as the interviewer.

● The three characters from the story are interviewed in turn about (i) why they want money, (ii) how they try to get (or keep) it, (iii) what they do (or plan to do) with it, and (iv) whether they find happiness through having it.

● When you are being interviewed, use your knowledge of the story to answer the questions asked. You may use your imagination to fill out your answers, as long as you stay in character.

c **By yourself**, write on one or both of the following topics:

(i) Show how at least **two** characters in *The Tinderbox* are driven by the desire for money. Describe what they do to get or keep it. On balance, does the story show that the search for riches is worth it?

(ii) Imagine that at some time in the future you win the National Lottery jackpot. Describe how you use the prize money, and explain your *reasons* for doing so.

THE SNOW QUEEN

A fairy tale told in seven stories

Look out for...
- how the devil's mirror breaks, and where its glass splinters fall.
- how Kai and Gerda become good friends.
- how Kai suddenly changes, and why he disappears from home.

The First Story, which concerns itself with a broken mirror and what happened to its fragments

All right, we will start the story; when we come to the end we shall know more than we do now.

Once upon a time there was a troll, the most evil troll of them all; he was called the devil. One day he was particularly pleased with himself, for he had invented a mirror which had the strange power of being able to make anything good or beautiful that it reflected appear horrid; and all that was evil and worthless seem attractive and worth while. The most beautiful landscape looked like spinach; and the kindest and most honourable people looked repulsive or ridiculous. They might appear to be standing on their heads, without any stomachs; and their faces would always be so distorted that you couldn't recognise them. A little freckle would spread itself out till it covered half a nose or a whole cheek.

'It is a very amusing mirror,' said the devil. But the most amusing part of it all was that if a good or a kind thought passed through anyone's mind the most horrible grin would appear on the face in the mirror.

COMMENTARY
The devil invents a magic mirror. In it, everything that is good is reflected as evil or ugly, and everything bad appears to be attractive.

troll: a mischievous dwarf
repulsive: disgusting
distorted: twisted, misshapen

It was so entertaining that the devil himself laughed out loud. All the little trolls who went to troll school, where the devil was headmaster, said that a miracle had taken place. Now for the first time one could see what humanity and the world really looked like – at least, so they thought. They ran all over with the mirror, until there wasn't a country or a person in the whole world that had not been reflected and distorted in it.

At last they decided to fly up to heaven to poke fun at the angels and God Himself. All together they carried the mirror, and flew up higher and higher. The nearer they came to heaven, the harder the mirror laughed, so that the trolls could hardly hold on to it; still, they flew higher and higher: upward towards God and the angels, then the mirror shook so violently from laughter that they lost their grasp; it fell and broke into hundreds of millions of billions and some odd pieces. It was then that it really caused trouble, much more than it ever had before. Some of the splinters were as tiny as grains of sand and just as light, so that they were spread by the winds all over the world. When a sliver like that entered someone's eye it stayed there; and the person, forever after, would see the world distorted, and only be able to see the faults, and not the virtues, of everyone around him, since even the tiniest fragment contained all the evil qualities of the whole mirror. If a splinter should enter someone's heart – oh, that was the most terrible of all! – that heart would turn to ice.

Some of the pieces of the mirror were so large that windowpanes could be made of them, although through such a window it was no pleasure to contemplate your friends. Some of the medium-sized pieces became spectacles – but just think of what would happen when you put on such a pair of glasses in order to see better and be able to judge more fairly. That made the devil laugh so hard that it tickled in his stomach, which he found very pleasant.

Some of the tiniest bits of the mirror were still flying about in the air. And now you shall hear about them.

sliver: a thin pointed piece
contemplate: look at, consider

COMMENTARY
The trolls fly up to heaven with the devil's mirror to make fun of God. They are laughing so much that they drop it. Splinters from the broken mirror pierce people's eyes and hearts all over the world.

The Second Story, which is about a little boy and a little girl

In a big city, where there live so many people and are so many houses that not every family can have a garden of its own and so must learn to be satisfied with a potted plant, there once lived a poor little girl and a poor little boy who had a garden a little bit larger than a flowerpot. They weren't brother and sister but loved each other as much as if they had been. Their parents lived right across from each other; each family had a little apartment in the garret, but the houses were so close together that the roofs almost touched. Between the two gutters that hung from the eaves and collected the water when it rained, there was only a very narrow space, and the two families could visit each other by climbing from one gable window to the other.

In front of the windows each family had a wooden box filled with earth, where herbs and other useful plants grew; but in each box there was also a little rose tree. The parents got the idea that, instead of setting the boxes parallel to their windows, they could set them across, so they reached from one window to the other. In that manner, the two gables were connected by a little garden. The peas climbed over the sides and hung down; and the little rose trees grew as tall as the windows and joined together, so that they looked like a green triumphal arch. The sides of the boxes were quite high and since the children could be relied upon not to climb over them, they were allowed to take their little wooden stools outside and sit under the rose trees; and there it was pleasant to play.

In winter that was not possible; then the windows were tightly closed and sometimes they would be covered by ice. Then the little children would heat copper coins on the stove and press them against the glass until the roundest of holes would melt in the ice; through each of these peeped the loveliest little eye: one belonged to a little boy and the other to a little girl. His name was Kai and hers was Gerda. In summer they had to take only a few steps to be together; but in the winter they had to run down and up so many stairs and across a yard covered by snowdrifts.

COMMENTARY
Two poor families live opposite each other in the same street. Their houses are so close together that they almost touch. There is no room for gardens; instead, they have window-boxes. The roses in them join together in an arch over the street.

One family has a son, Kai; the other a daughter, Gerda. They are already close friends.

garret: a top-floor room or attic
eaves: edges of the roofs
gable window: a window just below the roof

Kai: pronounced 'Kay'

'The white bees are swarming,' said the old Grandmother.

'Do they have a queen too?' asked Kai, for he knew that real bees have such a ruler.

'Yes, they have,' said the old woman. 'She always flies right in the centre of the swarm, where the most snowflakes are. She is the biggest of them all, but she never lies down to rest as the other snowflakes do. No, when the wind dies she returns to the clouds. Many a winter night she flies through the streets of the town and looks in through the windows; then they become covered by ice flowers.'

'Yes, I've seen that!' said first one child and then the other; and now they knew that what the Grandmother said was true.

'Could the Snow Queen come inside, right into our room?' asked the little girl.

'Let her come,' said Kai. 'I will put her right on top of the stove and then she will melt.'

The Grandmother patted his head and told them another story. But that night, as Kai was getting undressed, he climbed up on the chair by the window and looked out through his peephole. It was snowing gently; one of the flakes fell on the edge of the wooden box and stayed there; other snowflakes followed and they grew until they took the shape of a woman. Her clothes looked like the whitest gauze. It was made of millions of little star-shaped snowflakes. She was beautiful but all made of ice: cold, blindingly glittering ice; and yet she was alive, for her eyes stared at Kai like two stars, but neither rest nor peace was to be found in her gaze. She nodded toward the window and beckoned. The little boy got so frightened that he jumped down from the chair; and at that moment a shadow crossed the window as if a big bird had flown by.

The next day there was frost; but by noon the weather changed and it thawed. Soon it was spring again and the world grew green; the swallows returned to build their nests and the windows were opened. The little children sat in their boxes, above the eaves and high above all the other storeys of the houses.

white bees: snowflakes
gauze: thin, see-through fabric
beckoned: signalled Kai to come to her

COMMENTARY

On a stormy winter's day, the old Grandmother tells Kai and Gerda a folk-tale about the Snow Queen.

The same night, it is still snowing. Through his bedroom window Kai sees the Snow Queen. She is beautiful but has a cold, frightening gaze.

Soon the winter turns to spring. Kai forgets the Snow Queen.

The roses bloomed particularly marvellously that summer. The little girl had learned a psalm in which roses were mentioned in one of the verses; her own roses reminded her of it, and so she sang, and the boy joined her:

> In the valley where the roses be
> There the child Jesus you will see.

The two little children held each other's hands, kissed the flowers, and looked up into the blessed sunshine. Oh, these were lovely summer days, and it was ever so pleasant to sit under the little rose trees that never seemed to stop flowering.

One afternoon as Kai and Gerda sat looking at a picture book with animals and flowers in it – it was exactly five o'clock, for the bells in the church tower had just struck the hour – Kai said, 'Ouch, ouch! Something pricked my heart!' And then again, 'Ouch, something sharp is in my eye.'

The little girl put her arms around his neck and looked into his eyes but there was nothing to be seen. Still, it hurt and little Gerda cried out of sympathy.

'I think it is gone now,' said Kai. But he was wrong, two of the splinters from the devil's mirror had hit him: one had entered his heart and the other his eyes. You remember the mirror, it was that horrible invention of the devil which made everything good and decent look small and ridiculous, and everything evil and foul appear grand and worth while. Poor Kai, soon his heart would turn to ice and his eyes would see nothing but faults in everything. But the pain, that would disappear.

'Why are you crying?' he demanded. 'You look ugly when you cry. There is nothing the matter with me. Look!' he shouted. 'That rose up there has been gnawed by a worm; and look at that one, it is all crooked. They are ugly roses, as ugly as the boxes they grew in.' Then he kicked the sides of the box and tore off the two roses.

COMMENTARY

Kai's friendship with Gerda blossoms. One afternoon, as the friends are playing together, two splinters from the devil's mirror pierce Kai. One goes into his eye; the other enters his heart. Immediately, he starts to behave differently.

be: are to be found
gnawed: eaten up, destroyed

'What are you doing, Kai?' cried the little girl, and when Kai saw how frightened she was, he tore off yet another flower; and then climbed through the window into his parents' apartment, leaving Gerda to sit out there all alone.

Later, when she came inside with the picture book, he told her that picture books were for babies. And when the Grandmother told stories he would argue with her or – which was much worse – stand behind her chair with a pair of glasses on his nose and imitate her most cruelly. He did it so accurately that people laughed. Soon he learned to mimic everyone in the whole street. He had a good eye for their little peculiarities and knew how to copy them.

Everyone said, 'That boy has his head screwed on right!' But it was the splinters of glass that were in his eyes and his heart that made him behave that way; that, too, was why he teased little Gerda all the time – she who loved him with all her heart.

He did not play as he used to; now his games were more grown up. One winter day when snow was falling he brought a magnifying glass and looked at the snowflakes that were falling on his blue coat.

'Look through the glass, Gerda,' he said to his little playmate; and she did. Through the magnifying glass each snowflake appeared like a flower or ten-pointed star. They were, indeed, beautiful to see.

'Aren't they marvellous?' asked Kai. 'And each of them is quite perfect; they are much nicer than real flowers. They are all flawless as long as they don't melt.'

A little bit later he came by, with his sled on his back, and wearing his hat and woollen gloves. He screamed into Gerda's ear as loud as he could, 'I have been allowed to go down to the big square and play with the other boys!' And away he went.

Now down in the snow-covered square the most daring of the boys would tie their sleds behind the farmers' wagons. It was good fun and they would get a good ride. While they were playing, a big white sled drove into the square; the driver was clad in a white fur coat and a white fur hat. The sled circled the

peculiarities: odd ways of behaving
flawless: without fault
sled: sledge

COMMENTARY
Gerda is puzzled and upset by the change in Kai.

Winter returns and Kai grows tired of Gerda. Now he prefers to play with the older boys, hitching his sledge onto the back of farmers' wagons.

square twice and Kai managed to attach his little sled on to the back of the big one. He wanted to hitch a ride.

Away he went; the sled turned the corner and was out of the square. It began to go faster and faster, and Kai wanted to untie his sled, but every time he was about to do it, the driver of the big white sled turned and nodded so kindly to him that he didn't. It was as if they knew each other. Soon they were past the city gate; and the snow was falling so heavily that Kai could not see anything. He untied the rope but it made no difference, his little sled moved on as if it were tied to the big one by magic. They travelled along with the speed of the wind. Kai cried out in fear but no one heard him. The snow flew around him as he flew forward. Every so often his little sled would leap across a ditch and Kai had to hold on, in order not to fall off. He wanted to say his prayers, but all he could remember were his multiplication tables.

The snowflakes grew bigger and bigger until they looked like white hens that were running alongside him. At last the big sled stopped and its driver stood up and turned around to look at Kai. The fur hat and the coat were made of snow; the driver was a woman: how tall and straight she stood. She was the Snow Queen!

'We have driven a goodish way,' she said, 'but you look cold. Come, creep inside my bearskin coat.'

Kai got up from his own sled and walked over to the big one, where he sat down next to the Snow Queen. She put her fur coat around him, and it felt as if he lay down in a deep snowdrift.

'Are you still cold?' she asked, and kissed his forehead. Her kiss was colder than ice. It went right to his heart, which was already half made of ice. He felt as though he were about to die, but it hurt only for a minute, then it was over. Now he seemed stronger and he no longer felt how cold the air was.

'My sled, my sled, don't forget it!' he cried. And one of the white hens put it on her back and flew behind them. The Snow Queen kissed Kai once more, and then all memory of Gerda, the Grandmother, and his home disappeared.

'I shan't give you any more kisses,' she said, 'or I might kiss you to death.'

COMMENTARY
When a big white sledge drives into the city square, Kai ropes his own sledge to it. He goes faster and faster. Soon he finds himself far outside the city.

The driver of the white sleigh is the Snow Queen. Kai has been captured; he is now in her power. She seems to treat Kai kindly, though, and he soon stops being frightened.

Kai looked at the Snow Queen; he could not imagine that anyone could have a wiser or a more beautiful face; and she no longer seemed to be made of ice, as she had when he first saw her outside his window, the time she had beckoned to him. In his eyes she now seemed utterly perfect, nor did he feel any fear. He told her that he knew his multiplication tables, could figure in fractions, and knew the area in square miles of every country in Europe, and what its population was.

The Snow Queen smiled, and somehow Kai felt that he did not know enough. He looked out into the great void of the night, for by now they were flying high up in the clouds, above the earth. The storm swept on and sang its old, eternal songs. Above oceans, forests, and lakes they flew; and the cold winter wind whipped the landscape below them. Kai heard the cry of the wolves and the hoarse voice of the crows. The moon came out, and into its large and clear disk Kai stared all through the long winter night. When daytime came he fell asleep at the feet of the Snow Queen.

PAUSE FOR PLAYBACK:
Now look at the playback questions on page 71 before going on with your reading.

Look out for...
- **how Gerda sets out to look for Kai.**
- **what happens to Gerda when she meets the old lady.**
- **how the crow and the prince and princess try to help Gerda in her search.**

figure: do sums
void: empty space
eternal: age-old
disk: flat, circular object

COMMENTARY
The Snow Queen flies far away with Kai.

The Third Story: the flower garden of the old woman who knew magic

But how did little Gerda feel when Kai did not return? She asked everyone where he had gone and none could answer. The boys who had been in the square could only tell that they had seen him tie his little sled to the back of a big white sled that had driven out of the city gate.

No one knew were he had gone and little Gerda cried long and bitterly. As time passed people began to say that he must have died; probably he had drowned in the deep, dark river that ran close to the city. It was a long and dismal winter.

Finally spring came with warm sunshine.

'Kai is dead and gone!' sighed little Gerda.

'I don't believe that,' said the sunbeams.

'No, he is dead and gone,' she repeated, and asked the swallows if that were not true.

'We don't believe it either,' they answered; and at last little Gerda was convinced that Kai was not dead.

'I will put on my new red shoes, the ones Kai has never seen,' she said one day. 'And then I will go down to the river and ask it a few questions.'

It was early in the morning; she kissed the old Grandmother, who was still asleep, put on her new red shoes, and walked out through the city gate and down to the river.

'Is it true that you have taken my playmate? I will give you my new red shoes if you will give him back to me.'

She thought that the little waves nodded strangely; so she took her treasure, her new red shoes, and threw them out into the river. They struck the water not far from shore, and the little waves carried them back to her. It was as if the river did not want her little shoes since it had not taken Kai. This little Gerda did not realise, she thought that she just hadn't thrown them far enough out; therefore, she climbed into a rowing boat that lay among the reeds, stood up in its stern, and threw the shoes out over the water again. The

stern: back of the boat

COMMENTARY
Gerda is heartbroken to have lost her friend – especially when everyone says he must he dead. She will not believe that Kai is lost forever.

boat had not been moored and, by stepping into the stern, she loosened the bow from the sand and the rowing boat started to drift. Although she noticed it at once and turned around, prepared to leap up on to the bank, the boat was already several feet away from shore and she didn't dare jump.

The boat floated faster and faster downstream with the current. Poor Gerda was so frightened that she just sat down and cried. No one heard her except the sparrows and they could not carry her to shore. But they flew alongside the boat, twittering: 'We are here! We are here!' to comfort her.

The boat drifted down the river. Gerda sat perfectly still; she was in her stocking feet; the shoes followed the boat but they were far behind. The landscape was beautiful on both sides of the river. Beyond the banks, which were covered with flowers, there were meadows with cows and sheep grazing upon them; but there was not a human being to be seen anywhere.

'Maybe the river will carry me to where Kai is,' thought Gerda.

And that thought was a great comfort and she felt much happier. For hours she sat looking at the green shores; then the boat drifted past a cherry orchard; in the middle of it stood a strange little house with blue and green windows and a straw roof. Before the doors two wooden soldiers kept guard and presented arms when a boat glided by on the river.

Little Gerda, thinking that they were alive, waved and called; but naturally they did not answer. The current of the river carried the boat to the shore, and Gerda started to shout for help as loudly as she could. An old lady came out of the house; she had on a big broad-brimmed hat with the loveliest paintings of flowers on it.

'Poor little child!' she cried when she saw Gerda. 'How did you get out there on the river, all alone, and sail so far out into the wide world?' The old lady waded out till she could catch hold of the boat with her shepherd's crook and drew it into shore. Then she lifted Gerda out of the boat. The poor child was happy to be on dry land once again, but she was a little afraid of the old lady.

'Tell me who you are and how you have got into such a predicament.' the old woman asked.

---

moored: tied up
bow: front of the boat
presented arms: stood to attention
predicament: dangerous situation

COMMENTARY

All alone, Gerda sets out to search for Kai in a rowing boat. The river carries her faster and faster downstream. At the mercy of the river, Gerda is swept far beyond the city. Eventually she sees a cottage on the river bank. The old lady who lives there wades out and drags Gerda's boat to the shore. She seems kind, but Gerda is a little frightened of her.

Gerda told her everything and the old lady shook her head. When Gerda asked whether she had seen little Kai, all the old lady could say was that he hadn't gone by her house but that he probably would arrive there sooner or later. She told little Gerda not to be so sad but to come and eat some of her cherries and look at her flowers. They were prettier than any picture book, and every one of them could tell a story. The old lady took Gerda by the hand, opened the door to her little house, and led her inside.

The windows were placed high up, and the coloured glass gave a strange light to the room. On the table stood a bowl filled with the most delicious cherries, and Gerda ate as many of them as she could. While she ate, the old woman combed Gerda's hair with a gold comb and her hair curled prettily around her little rosebud face.

'I have longed so much for a little girl like you,' said the old woman. 'You just wait and see what good friends we shall become.'

While her hair was being combed, Gerda began to forget her playmate Kai more and more. The old lady knew witchcraft; but she was not an evil witch, she just liked to do a little magic for her own pleasure. She wanted little Gerda to stay with her very much; that was why she went with her shepherd's crook out into the garden and pointed it at all the rosebushes. Immediately, the sweet flowering bushes sank down into the earth and disappeared. One could not even see where they had been. Now she need not fear that when little Gerda saw the roses she would think of Kai and run away.

Then she took Gerda out into the garden and showed it to her. Oh, what a beautiful place it was! All the flowers imaginable were there; and all of them in full bloom, although they belonged to different seasons. Certainly no picture book could be as beautiful as they were. Gerda almost jumped for joy, and she played among them all day until the sun set behind the tall cherry trees. Then she was given the loveliest of beds with a red quilt stuffed with dried violets to cover herself; and there she slept, dreaming sweeter dreams than even a queen on her wedding night.

COMMENTARY
The old lady treats Gerda lovingly, like a daughter. Secretly, she plans to keep her for ever. So that Gerda will forget about her search for Kai, the old lady uses magic to make every rose in her garden disappear.

The next day she played in the warm sunshine with the flowers again; and in this manner many days went by. Gerda, at last, knew every flower in the garden, and though there were so many different kinds, there seemed to be one missing, but she did not know which it was.

One day as she was sitting looking at the old lady's grand hat, with its painted flowers, she saw among them a rose. The old woman had forgotten the one in her hat when she got rid of all the roses – that happens if you are absent-minded.

'What!' exclaimed Gerda. 'Are there no roses in the garden?' She ran about the garden, looking and searching, but nowhere did she find a rosebush. She felt so sad that she wept and her tears fell on the very plot of earth where a rose tree had grown. Through the earth, moistened by her tears, the tree shot upward again, blooming just as beautifully as when the old woman had made it vanish. Gerda kissed the flowers and thought of the roses at home and of little Kai.

'I have stayed here much too long,' she cried. 'I must find little Kai. Do you know where he is?' she asked the roses. 'Do you think that he is dead?'

'No, he is not dead,' answered the roses. 'We have been down under the earth, where the dead are, and Kai was not there.'

'Thank you,' said little Gerda. She asked the other flowers if they knew where Kai was.

Every flower stood in the warm sunshine and dreamed its own fairy tale; and that it was willing to tell, but none of them knew anything about Kai.

What story did the tiger lily tell her? Here it is:

'Can you hear the drum: boom…boom! It has only two beats: boom…boom. Listen to the woman's song of lament; hear the priest chant. The Hindu wife is standing on the funeral pyre, dressed in a long red gown. Soon the flames will devour her and her husband's body. She is thinking of someone who is standing among the mourners; his eyes burn even hotter than the flames that lick her feet, his flaming eyes did burn her heart with greater heat than those flames which soon will turn her body into ashes. Can the fire of a funeral pyre extinguish the flame that burns within the heart?'

tiger lily: an orange flower with black
    spots
lament: grief
funeral pyre: a fire for burning dead bodies
extinguish: put out

COMMENTARY
Gerda stays with the old lady for many months. One day, she remembers Kai when she sees a rose in the old lady's hat. Tearfully, Gerda asks the flowers in the garden if they know where Kai might be.

'That story I don't understand,' said little Gerda.

'Well, it is my fairy tale,' answered the tiger lily.

Next Gerda asked the honeysuckle; and this is what it said:

'High up above the narrow mountain road the old castle clings to the steep mountainside. Its ancient walls are covered by green ivy; the vines spread over the balcony where a beautiful young girl stands. No unplucked rose is fresher than she, no apple blossom, plucked and carried by the spring wind, is lighter or dances more daintily than she. Hear how her silk dress rustles. Will he not come soon?'

'Is that Kai you mean?' asked little Gerda.

'I tell only my own story, my own dream,' answered the honeysuckle.

Now it was the little daisy's turn:

'Between two trees a swing has been hung. Two sweet little girls, with dresses as white as snow and from whose hats green ribbons hang, lazily swing back and forth. Their brother, who is older than they are, is standing up behind them on the swing. He has his arms around the ropes so that he will not fall. In one hand he has a little bowl; in the other, a clay pipe. He is blowing soap bubbles. The swing glides, and the bubbles with their ever changing colours fly through the air. The last bubble clings to the pipe, then the breeze takes it. A little black dog, which belongs to the children, stands on its hind legs barking at the bubble and it breaks. Such is my song: a swing and a world of foam.'

'Your tale may be beautiful but you tell it so sadly, and you didn't mention Kai at all,' complained little Gerda. 'I think I will ask the hyacinth.'

'There were three beautiful sisters; they were so fine and delicate that they were almost transparent. One had on a red dress; the second, a blue; and the third, a white one. They danced, hand in hand, down by the lake; but they were not elves, they were real human children. The air smelled so sweet that the girls wandered into the forest. The sweet fragrance grew stronger. Three coffins appeared; and in them lay the three beautiful sisters. They sailed across the lake, and glow-worms flew through the air like little candles. Were the

COMMENTARY
The tiger lily, the honeysuckle and the daisy all answer Gerda. The stories they tell concern her search for Kai, but their meaning is too hard for her to understand.

dancing girls asleep or were they dead? The smell of the flowers said they were corpses, the bells at vespers ring for the dead.'

'Oh, you make me feel so sad,' said little Gerda. 'And the fragrance from your flowers is so strong that it makes me think of the poor dead girls. Is Kai dead too? The roses, who have been down under the earth, said that he wasn't.'

'Ding! dong!' rang the little hyacinth bells. 'We are not tolling for Kai, we do not know him. We are singing our own little song, the only one we know.'

Gerda approached a little buttercup that shone so prettily between its green leaves.

'You little sun, tell me, do you know where my playmate is?' she asked.

The buttercup's little shining face looked so trustfully back at her, but it too had only its own song to sing and it was not about Kai.

'Into a little narrow yard,' began the buttercup, 'God's warm sun was shining; it was the first spring day of the year. The sunbeams reflected against the white walls of the neighbour's house; nearby the first little yellow flower had unfolded itself. It was golden in the sunlight; the old grandmother brought her chair outside to sit in the warm sun. Her grandchild, the poor little servant maid, had come home for a short visit. She kissed her grandmother. There was gold in that kiss: the gold of the heart. Gold in the mouth, gold on the ground, and gold in the blessed sunrise. Now that was my little story,' said the buttercup.

'Oh, the poor Grandmother,' sighed little Gerda. 'She must be longing for me and grieving, as she did when little Kai disappeared. But I will soon go back home and bring little Kai with me. There is no point in asking any of the other flowers, each one only sings its own song.'

She tied her long dress up so that she could run fast, and away she went. The narcissus hit her leg smartly when she jumped over it and Gerda stopped. 'What, do you know something?' she asked, and bent down toward the flower.

'I can see myself, I can see myself,' cried the narcissus. 'High up in the garret lives the little ballerina; she stands on tiptoe and kicks at the world, for

vespers: evening prayers said in church
tolling: ringing for someone's death
narcissus: a white sweet-smelling flower –
  in Greek legend, Narcissus fell in love
  with his own reflection

COMMENTARY
The next flower to answer Gerda is the buttercup. Its story makes her think of the old Grandmother, pining for her to come home. This helps Gerda decide to escape from the old lady's cottage at all costs.

it is but a mirage. She pours a little water from the kettle on a piece of cloth; it is her corset that she is washing, for cleanliness is next to godliness. Her white dress is hanging in the corner; it has also been washed in the teakettle, then it was hung out on the roof to dry. Now she puts it on, and around her neck she ties a saffron-coloured kerchief; it makes the dress seem even whiter. She lifts one leg high in the air. She is bending her stem. I can see myself! I can see myself!'

'I don't care either to see you or to hear about you,' said Gerda angrily. 'Your story is a silly story,' and with those words she ran to the other end of the garden.

The door in the wall was closed; she turned the old rusty handle and it sprang open. Out went little Gerda, in her bare feet, out into the wide world. Three times she turned to look back but no one seemed to have noticed her flight.

At last she could not run any farther, and she sat down on a big stone to rest. She looked at the landscape; summer was long since over, it was late fall. Back in the old lady's garden, you could not notice the change in seasons, for it was always summer and the flowers of every season were in bloom.

'Goodness me, how much time I have wasted,' sighed Gerda. 'It is already autumn, I do not dare rest any longer,' and she got up and walked on. Her little feet hurt and she was tired. The leaves of the willow tree were all yellow, the water from the cold, fall mist dripped from it, as its leaves fell one by one. Only the blackthorn bush bore fruits now, and they are bitter. Oh, how sombre and grey seemed the wide world.

The Fourth Story, in which appear a prince and a princess

More and more often did Gerda have to rest. The ground was now covered with snow. A big crow landed near her; the bird sat there a long time, wriggling its head and looking at her. 'Caw...Caw!' he remarked, which in crow language means 'Good day.' He was kind and asked the girl why she

COMMENTARY
Without anyone trying to stop her, Gerda gets out of the garden through a door in its wall. She has no idea where in the world she is. However, she notices that a lot of time has passed; winter is coming on, and everywhere looks bleak.

mirage: optical illusion
saffron-coloured: orange
fall: autumn
sombre: sad and dreary

was out all alone in the lonely winter world.

The word 'alone' Gerda understood only too well; and she told the crow her story and asked him if he had seen little Kai.

The crow nodded most thoughtfully and said 'maybe, maybe!'

'Oh, he is alive!' screamed little Gerda, and almost squeezed the poor bird to death, while she kissed him.

'Be sensible, be sensible,' protested the crow. 'It may be little Kai I have seen; but if it is, then I am afraid he has forgotten you for the sake of the princess.'

'Does he live with a princess?' asked little Gerda.

'Yes, he does,' answered the crow, 'but are you sure you don't understand crow language? I much prefer speaking it.'

'No, I have never learned it; but Grandmother knows it, I wish now that she had taught it to me.'

'Never mind, it can't be helped,' said the crow. 'I shall do my best, which is a lot more than most people do,' and the crow told Gerda all that he knew:

'Now in this kingdom, where we are at present, there lives a princess who is immensely clever; she has read all the newspapers in the whole world and forgotten what was written in them, and that is the part that proves how intelligent she is. A few weeks ago, while she was sitting on the throne – and that, people say, is not such an amusing place to sit – she happened to hum a song which has as its chorus the line "Why shouldn't I get married?"

'"Why not, indeed?", thought the princess. "But if I am to get married it must be to a man who can speak up for himself." She didn't want anyone who just stood about looking distinguished, for such a fellow is boring. She called all her ladies in waiting and told them of her intention. They clapped their hands, and one of them said, "Oh, how delightful. I had such an idea myself just the other day." …Believe me, everything I tell you is true,' declared the crow. 'My fiancée is tame, she has the run of the castle and it is from her I got the story.' His fiancée was, naturally, another crow, for birds of a feather flock together.

'The newspapers were printed with a border of hearts and the princess'

immensely: tremendously
distinguished: grand
has the run of: is allowed to go
    anywhere in

COMMENTARY
A crow lands near Gerda and tells her he may have seen Kai. If it *is* him, he has forgotten Gerda and is married to a princess who rules the kingdom in this part of the world.

name on the front page. Inside there was a royal proclamation: any good-looking man, regardless of birth, could come to the castle and speak with the princess, and the one who seemed most at home there and spoke the best, she would marry.

'Believe me,' said the crow, and shook his head, 'as sure as I am sitting here, that proclamation got people out of their houses. They came thick and fast, you have never seen such a crowd. But neither the first nor the second day did the princess find anyone who pleased her. They could all speak well enough as long as they were standing in the street; but as soon they had entered the castle gates and saw the royal guards, in their silver uniforms, the young men lost their tongues. They didn't get them back, either, when they had to climb the marble stairs, lined with lackeys dressed in gold; or when they finally arrived in the grand hall with the great chandeliers and had to stand in front of the throne on which the princess sat. All they could do was repeat whatever she said; and that she didn't want to hear once more. One should think every one of them had had his tummy filled with snuff or had fallen into a trance. But as soon as they were down in the streets again they got their tongues back, and all they could do was talk.

There was a queue, so long that it stretched from beyond the city gate all the way up to the castle. I flew into town to have a look at it. Most of the men got both hungry and thirsty while they waited; the princess didn't even offer them a glass of lukewarm water. Some of the more clever ones had brought sandwiches, but they didn't offer any to their neighbours, for they thought: "Let him look hungry and the princess won't take him."

'But Kai! What about Kai?' asked Gerda. 'Did he stand in the queue too?'

'Don't be impatient. We are coming to him. Now the third day a little fellow arrived, he didn't have a carriage nor did he come on horseback. No, he came walking straight up to the castle. He was poorly dressed but had bright shining eyes like yours, and the most beautiful long hair.'

'That is Kai!' shouted little Gerda, and clapped her hands in joy.

'He had a little knapsack on his back,' continued the crow.

COMMENTARY
The crow tells Gerda how the princess chose her husband. All the handsome men in the kingdom were invited to be interviewed by her at her castle. Whoever spoke well and seemed most at ease would be considered for marriage.

After three days, says the crow, a poorly dressed young man walked up to the castle. Unlike others in the queue, he was not overcome by nerves.

proclamation: announcement
lackeys: servants
snuff: powdered tobacco sniffed through
  the nose

'It wasn't a knapsack,' interrupted Gerda. 'It was his sled.'

'Sled or knapsack, it doesn't matter much,' said the crow. 'I didn't look too closely at him. But this I know from my fiancée: when he entered the castle and saw the royal guards and all the lackeys, they didn't make him the least bit fainthearted. He nodded kindly to them and said, 'It must be boring to spend your life waiting on the stairs, I think I will go inside.' The big hall with its lighted candelabra, its servants carrying golden bowls, while courtiers stood around dressed in their very best, was impressive enough to take away the courage of even the bravest – and, on top of all that, the young man's boots squeaked something wicked – but he did not seem to notice either the elegant hall or his noisy boots.'

'It must be Kai,' said Gerda. 'His boots were new and I know they squeaked, I have heard them myself.'

'Well, squeak they did,' said the crow. 'But he walked right up to the princess, who was sitting on a pearl as big as a spinning wheel. Behind her stood all her ladies in waiting with their maids and their maids' maids; and all the gentlemen of the court with their servants and their servants' servants, each of whom, in turn, kept a boy. And the servants' servant's boy, who stood next to the door, always wore slippers and was so proud that one hardly dared look at him!'

'It must have been horrible!' Little Gerda shook her head. 'But Kai got the princess anyway?'

'If I hadn't been a crow, I would have taken her and that even though I am engaged. My fiancée tells me that he talks as well as I do when I talk crow language. He said that he hadn't come to propose marriage but only to find out whether she was as clever as everybody said she was. He was satisfied that what he heard was true and the princess was satisfied with him.'

'I am sure it was Kai, for he is so clever, he can work out fractions. Won't you take me to the castle.'

'That is easier said than done,' said the crow, and looked thoughtfully at Gerda. 'I will talk to my fiancée about it, she might know how we can do it.

candelabra: a large candlestick designed to
  hold a number of candles

COMMENTARY
Gerda is sure this *must* be Kai –
especially when the crow says that his
boots squeaked. She asks the crow to
help her get into the castle.

For I can tell you, it is not easy for a poor little girl like you to get into the castle.'

'But I will get in!' protested Gerda. 'As soon as Kai hears that I am here he will come and fetch me himself.'

'Wait here by the big stone,' commanded the crow, wriggled his head, and flew away.

The crow didn't return before dusk. 'Caw! Caw!' he said, and alighted on the stone. 'I bring you greetings from my fiancée, she sends you this little piece of bread. She took it in the kitchen where there is bread enough, and you must be hungry. It is quite impossible for you to enter the castle. You have bare feet; the guards in their silver uniforms and the lackeys in their golden ones won't allow it. But don't weep, we will get you in anyway. My fiancée knows where the key is kept to the back stairs, and they lead right up to the royal bedchamber.'

They entered the royal garden and watched the lights in the castle being extinguished, one by one. At last the crow led her to a little door in the rear of the castle that was half open. Little Gerda's heart beat both with fear and with longing, she felt as though she were doing something wrong; and yet all she wanted to do was to see whether it was little Kai who had won the princess. She was sure it must be he.

In her mind she saw his lively, clever eyes, his long hair; he was smiling as he did when they sat under the little rose trees at home. He would be happy to see her, and she would tell him of the long journey she had made for his sake. She would tell him, too, how sad everyone had become because he had gone, and how they all had missed him. She felt so happy and so fearful.

They had reached the stairs; a little lamp burned on a chest. In the middle of the floor stood a tame crow, twisting its head about and looking at her quizzically. Gerda curtsied as Grandmother had taught her to do.

'My fiancé has told me so many nice things about you. He has narrated your *vita* as it is called. I have found the story most touching! Will you take the lamp and I shall walk ahead and show the way.'

COMMENTARY

The crow thinks it will be difficult for Gerda to get into the castle, since she looks so poor and is bare-footed. However, he promises that his fiancée will try smuggling her in up the back stairs.

That night, Gerda sneaks into the castle. The crow's fiancée is waiting for her.

alighted: landed
quizzically: in a questioning way
narrated your vita: told me your life-story

'I think someone is coming,' whispered Gerda. There was a whirling, rushing sound; and on the wall were strange shadows of horses with flying manes, dogs and falcons, servants and hunters.

'Oh, they are only dreams,' said the crow. 'They have come to fetch their royal masters. That is only lucky for us; the easier it will be for you to have a good look at them while they are sleeping. But remember, when you gain honour and position, to be grateful and not forget those who helped you get it.'

'That is no way to talk,' grumbled the crow from the woods.

Now they entered the first of the great halls. The walls were covered with pink satin and decorated with artificial flowers. The shadows of the dreams reappeared, but they flew past so quickly that Gerda did not even get a chance to see whether Kai was mounted on one of the horses. Each hall they passed through was more magnificent than the one before it. At last they came to the royal bedchamber. The ceiling looked like the top of a large palm tree with glass leaves; from the centre of it eight ropes of pure gold hung down, attached to them were the two little beds that the royal couple slept in. Each bed was shaped like a lily; in the white lily slept the princess, and in the red lily the young man who had won her. Gerda peeped into it and saw a head of long brown hair. 'It is Kai!' she shouted in her joy. The dreams returned as fast as the wind and the young boy awoke.

He wasn't little Kai!

It was only the long brown hair they had in common, although he was young and handsome too. From the white lily bed the princess raised her head and asked what the commotion was about. Poor Gerda started to cry; and then between sobs, she told her story and explained how the crows had helped her.

'You poor thing!' said the prince. The princess said the same, and they did not scold the crows, on the contrary they praised them; although they warned them not to do it again. Still, they were to have a reward.

'Would you rather be free,' asked the princess 'or receive permanent positions as royal court crows, with permission to eat all leftovers?'

commotion: noisy disturbance
permanent positions: full-time jobs

COMMENTARY

Gerda is frightened by many strange shadows and eerie sounds, but the female crow says they are only dreams visiting the sleepers in the castle. Gerda reaches the royal bedchamber where the princess is sleeping with her newly-wed husband. With mixed feelings, Gerda sees that it is not Kai. The royal couple wake up.

Both the crows curtsied and said they preferred permanent positions. After all, they had to think of their old age. 'To be secure is better than to fly,' they said.

The prince got out of his bed and let Gerda sleep in it; he could hardly do more. She folded her little hands and thought, 'How good all animals and human beings are.' Then she closed her eyes and slept. The dreams returned and this time they looked like little angels; and one of them was drawing a sled behind her; and on it sat little Kai; and he nodded to Gerda. But that was only a dream and it was gone as soon as she awoke.

In the morning Gerda was dressed from head to toe in silk and velvet; and the little prince and princess begged her to stay with them. But she asked only for a little carriage and a horse and some boots, so that she could continue on her journey out in the wide world to find Kai.

She was given not only new boots but a muff as well, and good warm clothes. When she was ready to leave, a fine carriage of the purest gold drove up in front of the castle. The coat of arms of the princess was on the door, and not only was there a coachman to drive her, but a servant stood on the back of the carriage and two little soldiers rode in front. The prince and the princess themselves helped her into the carriage and wished her luck. Her friend, the crow from the woods, drove with her the first couple of miles. They sat beside each other, for the crow got sick if he had to ride sitting backward. The other crow stood at the gate and flapped her wings; she had had a headache since she had been given a permanent position, and besides she had overeaten. The carriage was lined with candy, and on the seat across from Gerda was a basket of fruit.

'Good-bye, good-bye!' shouted the little prince and princess; and Gerda wept, for she had grown fond of them, and the crow wept too. When they had driven a little way the crow said good-bye, and that was even harder to bear. He flew up into a tall tree and sat there waving with his black wings until he could no longer see the carriage that glistened as though it were made of sunlight.

COMMENTARY
After hearing Gerda's story, the royal couple kindly allow her to sleep in their room. She dreams happily of Kai.
Next day, Gerda leaves the castle. The prince and princess dress her like a queen, and she is given a golden carriage to ride in. She is sorry to say goodbye to people who have treated her so well – but the search for Kai must go on.

muff: a fur-covered wrap for warming the hands

PAUSE FOR PLAYBACK:
Now look at the playback questions on page 71 before going on with your reading.

Look out for…
● **what happens to Gerda when she meets the robbers.**
● **how Gerda is treated by the robber girl.**
● **why Gerda is able to travel to Lapland to look for Kai.**

The Fifth Story, which is about the robber girl

They were driving through a great dark forest, and the golden carriage shone like a flame right in the robbers' eyes, and they couldn't bear it.

'Gold! Gold!' they screamed as they came rushing out of the woods. They grabbed hold of the horses and killed the coachman, the servant, and the soldiers; then they dragged little Gerda out of the carriage.

'She is lovely and fat, I bet she has been fed on nuts,' said an old robber woman; she had a beard and eyebrows so big and bushy that they almost hid her eyes. 'She will taste as good as a lamb,' and the robber woman took a long shining knife from her belt; it was horrible to look at.

'Ouch!' screamed the old hag, for just at that moment she had been bitten in the ear by her own little daughter, whom she carried on her back. The child was such a wild and naughty creature that it was a marvel. 'Ouch!' the woman cried again, and missed her chance to kill Gerda.

'The girl is to play with me!' declared the little robber girl. 'But she is to give me her muff and her dress and sleep in my bed with me.' And just to make certain that her mother had understood her, she bit her again as hard as she could.

hag: ugly old woman

COMMENTARY
In a forest, Gerda is attacked by robbers. Her carriage is stolen; the coachman and servants are murdered. A robber woman is about to stab Gerda to death when her daughter – the robber girl – prevents her.

The robber woman turned and jumped into the air from the pain; and all the robbers laughed and said, 'Look how she dances with her brat.'

'I want to drive in the carriage,' cried the little robber girl, and she was allowed to, for she was terribly spoiled. She and Gerda sat inside the carriage while it was being driven along little paths that brought it deeper and deeper into the forest. The little robber girl was as tall as Gerda but much stronger, and her skin had been tanned by the sun. Her eyes were almost black and looked sad. She put her arms around Gerda and said, 'I won't allow them to kill you, so long as you don't make me angry. You must be a princess?'

'No, I am not,' answered Gerda, and then she told her whole story and how much she loved little Kai.

The robber girl looked very seriously at her, nodded her head, and said: 'I won't allow them to kill you even if I do get angry at you. I will do it myself.' Then she dried Gerda's eyes and put her own hands inside the warm soft muff.

At last the carriage stopped; they had come to the robber castle. The walls were cracked and the windows were broken. Crows and ravens flew in and out of the big holes in the tower. Big dogs ran about in the courtyard; they looked ferocious enough to be able to eat human beings; they sprang up in the air but they didn't bark, that wasn't allowed.

In the middle of the great hall a fire burned. The smoke drifted up among the blackened rafters; how it ever got out was its own business. A big copper kettle filled with soup hung over the fire, and next to it, on spits, hares and rabbits were being roasted.

'You are going to sleep with me, over here among all my little pet animals,' said the little robber girl, and dragged Gerda over to a corner of the hall, where there lay some straw and some blankets. Above them, on poles, sat about a hundred doves; they were asleep, but a couple opened their eyes and turned their heads when the little girls came.

'They are all mine,' said the girl, and grabbed one of them by its legs. The dove flapped its wings. 'Kiss it,' demanded the robber girl, and shoved the frightened bird right up into Gerda's face.

COMMENTARY

The robber girl hears the story of Gerda's search for Kai. She promises to protect her from being killed and eaten.

They arrive at the robber castle. It is a dirty, tumbledown place, very different from the castle Gerda has just left.

brat: badly-behaved child
spits: metal bars for cooking meat over an open fire

'Up there are two wood pigeons,' the robber girl explained as she pointed to a recess in the wall, high above them, that had been turned into a cage by a few wooden bars. 'They would fly away if they could, but they can't.'

'Here is my old sweetheart, bah!' She took hold of the antlers of a reindeer that stood tied near her bed and gave them a hard pull. 'One has got to hold on to him too, or he would leap away. Every evening I tickle his throat with my sharp knife, that frightens him.' The little girl pulled a knife out from a crack in the wall and let its sharp point glide around the reindeer's neck; the animal backed as far away as it could, in terror. That made the little robber girl laugh; and she pulled Gerda down into her bed.

'Do you sleep with your knife?' asked Gerda, frightened.

'I always sleep with the knife,' answered the little robber girl. 'One never knows what might happen. But tell me again the story of little Kai and why you have gone out into the wide world.' Gerda told her story once more, and the wood pigeons, up in their cage, cooed; the doves were all asleep. The little robber girl put one of her arms around Gerda – in her other hand, she kept her knife – and fell asleep. She snored loudly.

Poor Gerda didn't dare close her eyes; she didn't know whether she was going to live or die. The robbers all sat around the fire and sang while they drank. The little girl's mother was so drunk that she turned a somersault. Oh, it was a pretty sight for a little girl to see!

Suddenly one of the wood pigeons cooed, 'We have seen little Kai. A white hen carried his sled. He sat in the Snow Queen's sled when she flew low over the forest. We had just come out of our eggs and she breathed on us; all the other young ones died. We, alone, survived. Coo! Coo!'

'What is it you are saying?' cried Gerda. 'Where was the Snow Queen going? Do you know?'

'I suppose she went to Lapland, where there always are snow and ice, but ask the reindeer that stands tied by your bed.'

'Oh yes, ice and snow are always there; it is a blessed place,' sighed the reindeer. 'There one can jump and run about freely in the great, glittering

COMMENTARY

The robber girl shows Gerda her pets: doves, wood pigeons and a reindeer. She falls asleep with her knife in one hand and an arm thrown round Gerda. The adult robbers get drunk and rowdy, again putting Gerda in fear of her life. She finds it impossible to sleep.

Lying awake, Gerda hears a wood pigeon say he has seen Kai flying in the Snow Queen's sledge. She is probably heading for her castle in Lapland, near to the North Pole.

recess: an alcove set into the walk

valleys. The Snow Queen keeps a summer tent there, but her castle is far to the north, near the pole, on an island called Spitsbergen.'

'Oh, Kai, little Kai!' mumbled Gerda.

'Lie still,' commanded the robber girl, 'or I will slit open your stomach!'

In the morning Gerda told her what she had heard from the wood pigeons. The little robber girl looked quite solemn, then nodded her head and said, 'I am sure it is he, I am sure.' Then she turned to the reindeer and asked him if he knew where Lapland was.

'Who should know that better than I?' answered the poor animal 'There I was born, there I have run across the great snow fields.' And his eyes gleamed, recollecting what he had lost.

'Listen,' whispered the little robber girl to Gerda. 'All the men are gone. Only Mama is here and she won't leave; but in a little while she will take a drink from the big bottle and then she will take a nap. And then...I will help you!'

She jumped out of bed, ran over and threw her arms around her mother, pulled her beard, and said, 'Oh my own sweet billy goat, good morning!'

The mother tweaked her daughter's nose, so that it turned both red and blue, but it was all done out of love.

When the mother had drunk from the big bottle, she lay down for her midmorning nap; then the robber girl spoke to the reindeer: 'I would have loved to tickle your throat for many a day yet, for you look so funny when I do it. But never mind, I will let you loose so that you can run back to Lapland; but you are to take the little girl with you and bring her to the Snow Queen's palace where her playmate is. I know you have heard everything she said, for you are always eavesdropping.'

The reindeer leaped into the air out of pure joy. The robber's daughter lifted Gerda up on the animal's back and tied her on so she wouldn't fall off; and she even gave her a little pillow to sit on. 'I don't really care about your boots, you need them,' she said. 'It is cold where you are going. But the muff I am keeping, for it is so soft and nice. But you shan't freeze, I will give you my

COMMENTARY

When morning comes, the robber girl agrees to let her reindeer – who was born in Lapland – take Gerda there. The adult robbers are in a drunken sleep. Secretly, the robber girl unties her reindeer and gives Gerda food and warm clothes.

recollecting: remembering
tweaked: pulled, twisted
eavesdropping: listening in secret

mother's great big mittens; they will keep you warm all the way up to your elbows. Here, put them on! Now your hands look as ugly as my mother's.'

Gerda cried from happiness and relief.

'I don't like all your tears,' scolded the little robber girl. 'You should look happy now. Here are two loaves of bread and a ham, so you won't go hungry,' she said as she tied the bread and ham on the back of the reindeer; then she opened the door and called all the big dogs in. She cut the rope that tethered the reindeer and said in parting, 'Run along, but take good care of the little girl!'

Gerda waved good-bye with her great big mittens, and away they went, through the forest and across the great plains, as fast as they could. They heard the wolves howl and the ravens cry; and suddenly the sky was all filled with light.

'There are the old northern lights,' said the reindeer. 'Look how they shine!'

Still they went on both day and night: farther and farther north.

The bread was eaten and the ham was eaten; and then they were in Lapland.

PAUSE FOR PLAYBACK:
Now look at the playback questions on page 72 before going on with your reading.

---

tethered: tied up
northern lights: a group of bright stars in
    the northernmost sky

COMMENTARY
Soon Gerda is free – and travelling on the reindeer, back to Lapland.

Look out for...
- **how the Lapp woman and the Finnish woman help Gerda to find the Snow Queen's palace.**
- **how Kai and Gerda are reunited.**
- **what happens to the two friends on their way home.**

The Sixth Story: the Lapp woman and the Finnish woman

They stopped before a little cottage; it was a wretched little hovel: the roof went all the way down to the ground and the doorway was so low that you had to creep through it on all fours. The only person at home was an old Lapp woman who was busy frying some fish over an oil lamp. The reindeer told her Gerda's story; but first he had told his own, because he thought that was more interesting. Poor Gerda was so cold that she couldn't even talk.

'Oh you poor things!' said the Lapp woman. 'You have far to go yet. It is more than a hundred miles from here to the camp of the Snow Queen. She amuses herself by shooting fireworks off every night. I shall give you an introduction to the Finnish woman who lives up there. She knows more about it all than I do and will be able to help you. Paper I have none of, so I will write on a dried codfish.'

When little Gerda had eaten and was warm again, the Lapp woman wrote a few words on a dried codfish and told Gerda not to lose it. Then she tied her on the reindeer's back again and away they ran.

Whish...whish...it said up in the sky as the northern lights flickered and flared; they were the Snow Queen's fireworks. At last they came to the Finnish woman's house; they had to knock on the chimney, for the door was so small they couldn't find it.

Goodness me, it was hot inside! The Finnish woman walked around almost naked. She pulled off both Gerda's boots and her mittens so that the heat

COMMENTARY
Gerda arrives at the Lapp woman's cottage. She is still a hundred miles from the palace of the Snow Queen. Gerda is given an introduction to the Finnish woman; then she continues her journey north.

hovel: a small house

would not be unbearable for her. The reindeer got a piece of ice to put on its head. Then the Finnish woman read what was written on the codfish; she read it three times and then she knew it by heart. The fish she put in the pot that was boiling over the fire. It could be eaten, and she never wasted anything. The reindeer told first of his own adventures and then of Gerda's. The Finnish woman squinted her intelligent eyes but didn't utter a word.

'You are so clever,' said the reindeer finally. 'I know you can tie all the winds of the world into four knots on a single thread. If the sailor loosens the first knot he gets a fair wind; if he loosens the second a strong breeze; but if he loosens the third and the fourth knots, then there's such a storm that the trees in the forest are torn up by the roots. Won't you give this little girl a magic drink so that she gains the strength of twelve men and can conquer the Snow Queen?'

'The strength of twelve men,' laughed the Finnish woman. 'Yes, I should think that would be enough.' Then she walked over to a shelf and took down a roll of skin which she spread out on the table. Strange words were written there, and the Finnish woman read and studied till the perspiration ran down her forehead.

The reindeer begged her again to help little Gerda; and Gerda looked up at her with eyes filled with tears. The Finnish woman winked, then drew the reindeer into a corner, where she whispered to him while she gave him another piece of ice for his head.

'Little Kai is in the Snow Queen's palace and is quite satisfied with being there; he thinks it is the best place in the whole world. This is because he has got a sliver of glass in his heart and two grains of the same in his eyes. As long as they are there he will never be human again, and the Snow Queen will keep her power over him.'

'But can't you give Gerda some kind of power so that she can take out the glass?' asked the reindeer.

'I can't give her any more power than she already has! Don't you understand how great it is? Don't you see how men and animals must serve

by heart: word for word

COMMENTARY
At the Finnish woman's house, the reindeer begs her to help Gerda conquer the Snow Queen. The Finnish woman has magic powers, but she says they are not strong enough to break the Snow Queen's hold over Kai. Only Gerda herself can do that.

her; how else could she have come so far, walking on her bare feet? But she must never learn of her power; it is in her heart, for she is a sweet innocent child. If she herself cannot get into the Snow Queen's palace and free Kai from the glass splinters in his eyes and his heart, how can we help her? Two miles from here begin the gardens of the Snow Queen. Carry Gerda there and set her down by the bush with the red berries, then come right back here and don't stand about gossiping.' The Finnish woman lifted Gerda back on the reindeer's back, and he ran as fast as he could.

'I don't have my boots on, and I forgot my mittens,' cried Gerda when she felt the cold making her naked feet smart. But the reindeer did not dare return. He ran on until he came to the bush with the red berries. There he put Gerda down and kissed her on her mouth; two tears ran down the animal's cheeks; then he leaped and ran back to the Finnish woman as fast as he could.

There stood poor Gerda, barefooted and without mittens on, in the intense arctic cold. She entered the Snow Queen's garden and ran as fast as she could in the direction of the palace. A whole regiment of snowflakes advanced against her. They had not fallen from the sky, for that was cloudless and illuminated by northern lights. The snowflakes flew just above the snow-covered earth; and as they came nearer they grew in size. Gerda remembered how they had looked when seen through a magnifying glass, but these were even bigger and horrible to look at. They were the Snow Queen's guard. And what strange creatures they were! Some of them looked like ugly little porcupines, others like bunches of snakes all twisted together, and some like little bears with bristly fur. All of the snowflakes were brilliantly white and terribly alive.

Little Gerda stopped and said her prayers. It was so cold that she could see her own breath; it came like a fine white smoke from her mouth, then it became more and more solid and formed itself into little angels that grew as soon as they touched the ground; all of them had helmets on their heads and shields and spears in their hands. When Gerda had finished saying her prayers a whole legion of little angels stood around her. They threw their spears at the

COMMENTARY

The way for Gerda to free Kai is to use the strength of love she has for him in her heart, the Finnish woman tells the reindeer.

The reindeer takes Gerda to the edge of the Snow Queen's garden. Still barefoot and now on her own, she battles on through the thickening snow. She prays for strength. Her prayer is answered: a troop of angels help her to pass safely through the Snow Queen's guards.

smart: sting
advanced: moved like an army

snow monsters, and they splintered into hundreds of pieces. Little Gerda walked on unafraid, and the angels caressed her little feet and hands so she did not feel the cold.

But now we must hear what happened to little Kai. He was not thinking of Gerda – and even if he had been, he could not have imagined that she could be standing right outside the palace.

The Seventh Story: what happened in the Snow Queen's palace and afterwards

The walls of the palace were made of snow, and the windows and doors of the sharp winds; it contained more than a hundred halls, the largest several miles long. All were lighted by the sharp glare of the northern lights; they were huge, empty, and terrifyingly cold. Here no one had ever gathered for a bit of innocent fun; not even a dance for polar bears, where they might have walked on their hind legs in the manner of man and the wind could have produced the music. No one had ever been invited in for a little game of cards, with something good to eat and a bit of not too malicious gossip; nor had there ever been a tea party for young white lady foxes. No, empty, vast, and cold was the Snow Queen's palace.

The northern lights burned so precisely that you could tell to the very second when they would be at their highest and their lowest points. In the middle of that enormous snow hall was a frozen lake. It had cracked into thousands of pieces and every one of them was shaped exactly like all the others. In the middle of the lake was the throne of the Snow Queen. Here she sat when she was at home. She called the lake the Mirror of Reason, and declared that it was the finest and only mirror in the world.

Little Kai was blue – indeed, almost black – from the cold; but he did not feel it, for the Snow Queen had kissed all feeling of coldness out of him, and his heart had almost turned into a lump of ice. He sat arranging and rearranging pieces of ice into patterns. He called this the Game of Reason; and because of the splinters in his eyes, he thought that what he was doing was of

caressed: stroked
malicious: nasty, unkind

COMMENTARY

Inside the ice palace, the atmosphere is frighteningly cold and deathly. Kai is seated in the middle of an ice lake, near the Snow Queen's throne. She has frozen the boy's heart so powerfully that all his human feelings are numbed. But because the devil's splinters are still in his eyes and heart, Kai does not know that he is unable to feel normal emotions.

great importance, although it was no different from playing with wooden blocks, which he had done when he could hardly talk.

He wanted to put the pieces of ice together in such a way that they formed a certain word, but he could not remember exactly what that word was. The word that he could not remember was 'eternity.' The Snow Queen had told him that if he could place the pieces of ice so that they spelled that word, then he would be his own master and she would give him the whole world and a new pair of skates; but, however much he tried, he couldn't do it.

'I am going to the warm countries,' the Snow Queen had announced that morning. 'I want to look into the boiling black pots.' By 'black pots,' she meant the volcanoes, Vesuvius and Etna. 'I will chalk their peaks a bit. It will do them good to be refreshed; ice is pleasant as a dessert after oranges and lemons.'

The Snow Queen flew away and Kai was left alone in the endless hall. He sat pondering his patterns of ice, thinking and thinking; he sat so still one might have believed that he was frozen to death.

Little Gerda entered the castle. The winds began to whip her face, and could have cut it, but she said her prayers and they lay down to sleep. She came into the vast, empty, cold hall; then she saw Kai!

She recognised him right away, and ran up to him and threw her arms around him, while she exclaimed jubilantly: 'Kai, sweet little Kai. At last I have found you.'

But Kai sat still and stiff and cold; then little Gerda cried and her tears fell on Kai's breast. The warmth penetrated to his heart and melted both the ice and the glass splinter in it. He looked at her and she sang the psalm they had once sung together:

> Our roses bloom and fade away,
> Our infant Lord abides alway.
> May we be blessed his face to see
> And ever little children be.

COMMENTARY

The Snow Queen flies away to freeze volcanoes. Kai is left alone.

Gerda gets inside the ice palace. At the sight of Kai, she cries with joy. Her loving tears melt his heart and wash the devil's splinters from his eyes. He becomes human again.

eternity: an endless length of time
pondering: thinking deeply about, puzzling over
jubilantly: joyfully

Kai burst into tears and wept so much that the grains of glass in his eyes were washed away. Now he remembered her and shouted joyfully: 'Gerda! Sweet little Gerda, where have you been so long? And where have I been?' Kai looked about him. 'How cold it is, how empty, and how huge!' And he held on to Gerda, who was so happy that she was both laughing and crying at the same time. It was so blessed, so happy a moment that even the pieces of ice felt it and started to dance; and when they grew tired they lay down and formed exactly that word for which the Snow Queen had promised Kai the whole world and a new pair of skates.

Gerda kissed him on his cheeks and the colour came back to them. She kissed his eyes and they became like hers. She kissed his hands and feet, and the blue colour left them and the blood pulsed again through his veins. He was well and strong. Now the Snow Queen could return, it did not matter, for his right to his freedom was written in brilliant pieces of ice.

They took each other by the hand and walked out of the great palace. They talked of Grandmother, and the roses that bloomed on the roof at home. The winds were still; and as they walked, the sun broke through the clouds. When they reached the bush with the red berries the reindeer was waiting there for them. He had brought another young reindeer with him and her udder was bursting with milk. The two children drank from it and the reindeer kissed them. Then they rode on the backs of the reindeer to the home of the Finnish woman, where they got warm, were given a good meal and instructions for the homeward journey.

They visited the Lapp woman. She had sewn warm clothes for them and was getting her sled ready.

The two reindeer accompanied them to the border of Lapland. There the green grass started to break through the snow and they could not use the sled any longer. They said good-bye to the reindeer and to the Lapp woman. Soon they heard the twitter of the first birds of spring and in the woods the trees were budding.

They met a young girl wearing a red hat and riding a magnificent horse.

COMMENTARY

The Snow Queen is now powerless to keep Kai imprisoned. Gerda's innocent kisses are stronger than her evil ones. Kai rides away with Gerda on the reindeer. On the way home they meet the Finnish woman, the Lapp woman and the robber girl.

Gerda recognised the animal, for it was one of the horses that had drawn her golden carriage. The girl had two pistols stuck in her belt; she was the little robber girl, who had got tired of staying at home and now was on her way out into the wide world. She recognised Gerda immediately and the two of them were so happy to see each other.

'You are a fine one,' she said to Kai, 'running about as you did. I wonder if you are worth going to the end of the world for?' Gerda touched her cheek and asked her if she knew what had happened to the prince and princess. 'They have gone travelling in foreign lands,' answered the robber girl.

'And what about the crow?'

'The crow is dead,' said the girl. 'His tame fiancée has become a widow, she wears a black wool thread around her leg. She thinks mourning becomes her, but it is all nonsense. But tell me what happened to you and how you managed to find him!'

And both Gerda and Kai told her everything that had happened to them.

'Well, the end was as good as the beginning,' said the robber girl, and took each of them by the hand and promised that if she ever came through the town where they lived she would come and visit them. Then she rode away out into the world; and Kai and Gerda walked hand in hand homeward.

It was really spring. In the ditches the little wild flowers bloomed. The churchbells were ringing. Now they recognised the towers; they were approaching their own city and the home they had left behind.

Soon they were walking up the worn steps of the staircase to the old Grandmother's apartment. Nothing inside it had changed. The clock said 'Tick-tack...' and the wheels moved. But as they stepped through the doorway they realised that they had grown: they were no longer children.

The roses were blooming in the wooden boxes and the window was open. There were the little stools they used to sit on. Still holding each other's hands, they sat down, and all memory of the Snow Queen's palace and its hollow splendour disappeared. The Grandmother sat in the warm sunshine,

becomes her: suits her

COMMENTARY
The robber girl has left home. Like Gerda, she is making her own way in the world.

Back in their home city, Kai and Gerda find that nothing has altered – except themselves. All their adventures have changed them from children to grown-ups.

reading aloud from her Bible: 'Whosoever shall not receive the Kingdom of Heaven as a little child shall not enter therein.'

Kai and Gerda looked into each other's eyes and now they understood the words from the psalm.

> Our roses bloom and fade away,
> Our infant Lord abides alway.
> May we be blessed his face to see
> And ever little children be

There they sat, the two of them, grownups; and yet in their hearts children, and it was summer: a warm glorious summer day!

PAUSE FOR PLAYBACK:
Now look at the playback questions on page 72.

Whosoever shall not receive…therein: no one can be a good Christian unless they are as free from sin as a young child
abides alway: Jesus gave us the gift of eternal life

COMMENTARY
Kai and Gerda recognise their love for each other, sitting again by the roses that are now in full bloom. The old Grandmother reads aloud from her Bible. It tells them that it is the innocence and loving kindness in their hearts which has brought them safely home.

Study guide

PAGES 37 to 44:

- ➤ Glance back to *The First Story*. Get clear in your mind exactly what the devil's mirror does.
- ➤ The Snow Queen first appears in *The Second Story*. Re-read the descriptions of her on pages 40 to 44. What are your impressions of her?
- ➤ How does Kai's behaviour change when splinters from the devil's mirror pierce his eye and heart?
- ➤ Why do you think the Snow Queen wants to capture Kai? Where do you imagine she is taking him?

Now return to reading the story on page 44

PAGES 44 to 58:

- ➤ Would you say that the old lady helps or hinders Gerda in her search for Kai – or does she do both?
- ➤ Re-read the stories that the tiger lily, the honeysuckle and the daisy tell (pages 48 to 49). Can you see any ways in which they might apply to Kai and Gerda?
- ➤ Why does Gerda think that the princess's husband must be Kai? What do you imagine her feelings are when she finds she is wrong?
- ➤ Look back over what the crow says and does. How would you sum up his character?

Now return to reading the story on page 58

PAGES 58 to 62:

➤ In *The Fifth Story*, Gerda twice comes close to death. Whereabouts does this happen? What prevents her from being killed?
➤ Think about the way the robber girl treats Gerda. Would you say she is kind to her? Why do you think she decides to help Gerda get to Lapland?
➤ How would you describe the robber castle, and the people who live there, to someone who hasn't read this story? What are the biggest differences between the robber castle and the princess's castle in *The Fourth Story*?
➤ How close do you imagine Gerda now is to finding Kai – if she is going to find him at all?

Now return to reading the story on page 63

PAGES 63 to 70:

➤ Why is the Finnish woman not able to give Gerda 'more power than she already has' (page 64) to defeat the Snow Queen?
➤ Imagine you are Gerda. What feelings are you likely to have as you enter the ice palace and look around you?
➤ What puzzle has the Snow Queen given Kai to do? Why do you think he fails to solve it?
➤ If you had to tell a younger person *why* Gerda manages to break the spell on Kai, how would you explain it?

REVIEWING THE WHOLE STORY: SUGGESTED ACTIVITIES

1 Find Kai: a board game

Follow the stages of Gerda's search to find Kai. Note down all the things that help and hinder her on her journey. Then make a board game based on Gerda's adventures.

When it is finished, your board game will be able to be played by other people. It will also show:

- what happens to Gerda;

- who she meets;

- the main obstacles she comes up against;

- how she gets help from different people;

- how she finds Kai in the end.

How to work

a **In a group**, make a note chart to show the things that help and hinder Gerda, from the time she sets out in the boat to the time she reaches the Snow Queen's palace. Do it like this:

Helps Gerda	Hinders Gerda
Old woman — stops Gerda from being swept away by the river (page 46)	Old woman — tries to keep Gerda, which wastes a lot of her time (page 47)
Roses — tell Gerda that Kai isn't dead (page 48)	Crow — makes Gerda think Kai married the princess (page 53)

You should end up with at least six things in each column.

b On a large sheet of paper, draw the outline of a rectangle. Fill it with squares, numbered from 1 (the start of the journey) to 50 (Gerda's discovery of Kai). This is the 'grid' of your game.

c   Sketch onto your grid the 'map' of Gerda's journey. How you do this is up to you. It will look better if the places Gerda passes through, and the people she meets, are not just names but also *illustrated* in colour.

d   Now decide between you:

- the worst moments of her journey;

- the most fortunate things that happen on her journey.

Invent penalties for the worst moments. For example: *Gerda is captured by robbers who threaten to eat her – Go back six squares.*

Invent bonuses for the most fortunate things that happen. For example: *The reindeer is allowed to take Gerda to Lapland – Move forward to square 45.*

e   Talk about **how to play** your board game. You will need to think of things like:

- how many players can play at one time;

- what they need to do so (for example, counters, dice, etc.);

- how to start play;

- the rules of the game;

- how to win.

f   **By yourself**, draft and write a short booklet called ***Find Kai: how to play***. Set it out as simply and clearly as you can. When you are giving instructions about the rules, you should *not* use illustrations.

As you plan and write, bear in mind that the purpose of the booklet is:

- to explain to someone of your own age the object of the game;

- to explain how to use the board;

- to explain the rules of play.

g   **In your group**, try playing your game. If all goes well, invite another group to have a go while you play *their* game. If you find problems, discuss how to put them right before you ask others to play.

2 Kai's changes

a   **By yourself**, re-read *The First Story*. Remind yourself of what happens to people who are pierced by splinters from the devil's mirror.

b   **With a partner**, take turns to read aloud the first section of *The Second Story*. Stop when you come to: 'Kai said, "Ouch, ouch! Something pricked my heart!" And then again, "Ouch, something sharp is in my eye".' (page 41).

c   Working together, talk about the ways in which Kai's behaviour changes after this point. To help you, read on into *The Second Story* until you come to the sentence beginning 'He screamed into Gerda's ear as loud as he could…' (page 42).

d   **By yourself**, make a 'changes chart' to show:

● the sort of person Kai was, and how he behaved, before being pierced by the splinters;

● the sort of person Kai becomes, and how he behaves, after he is pierced by the splinters.

Do it like this:

Before	**After**
Very friendly and loving towards Gerda	Very rude and insulting towards Gerda

Include at least five changes on your chart.

e   Use what you have put on your chart to join in a **class discussion** about the changes that take place in Kai's character.

f   **By yourself**, write an account of how the devil's splinters make Kai into a completely different person from the one he was before.

3 A character ladder

During the story, Gerda meets some people who turn out to be good and helpful to her. Some that she meets turn out to be quite the opposite. Others come somewhere in between.

a   **As a class**, talk about where the following characters would stand on a Good and Bad Ladder with ten rungs:

   ● The old lady in *The Third Story*;

   ● The crow in *The Fourth Story*;

   ● The prince and princess in *The Fourth Story*;

   ● The little robber girl in *The Fifth Story*;

   ● The Finnish woman in *The Sixth Story*;

b   Give detailed reasons for deciding where to put each character on the ladder. There is no need to agree with everyone else, as long as you give *evidence* from the story to back up what you think.

c   When your discussion is over, draw **by yourself** a large 'character ladder'. Put the names of each character you have talked about where *you* think he/she belongs. Do this on the right-hand side of the ladder, as follows:

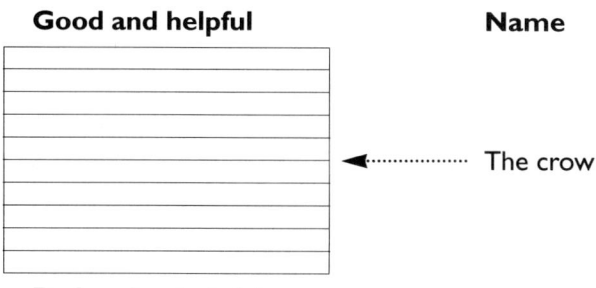

d   **By yourself**, write a description of whichever *two* characters on the ladder you have found most interesting. Bring out: (i) the sort of personality they have, (ii) how they treat Gerda, and (iii) why they appear on your ladder where they do.

   If you wish, include drawings of your two characters to show how you imagine they look.

4 | Colder than ice

a **By yourself**, re-read these three parts of the story:

- The old Grandmother's account of who the Snow Queen is (*The Second Story* – page 40).

- The description of how the Snow Queen makes off with Kai (*The Second Story* – pages 42 to 44).

- The description of the Snow Queen's palace in the first two paragraphs of *The Seventh Story* – page 66.

b **In a group**, talk about what Hans Andersen wants us to think about the Snow Queen by answering these questions:

- When the Snow Queen takes Kai into her sled, is she more kind to him than cruel – or more cruel to him than kind?

- What evidence does the story give that the Snow Queen puts some kind of spell on Kai? Does she ever remove it?

- In character, how is the Snow Queen like the palace where she lives?

- By the end of the story, is the Snow Queen victorious – or has she been defeated? How do you know?

- What is the importance of the Snow Queen in the story as a whole?

5 | Your own magic mirror story

Imagine that, for just one day, you have a magic mirror like the one in *The Snow Queen*. Describe your day's adventures.

Before beginning to plan your story, re-read pages 37 to 38. Notice the sentence: 'Some of the medium-sized pieces became spectacles – but just think of what would happen when you put on such a pair of glasses in order to see better and be able to judge more fairly.'

In *The Snow Queen*, it is the devil who has the magic mirror. However, it is possible for you to use it for 'good' purposes as well as to make mischief. This is for you to decide.

THE NIGHTINGALE

Look out for...
- the way everyone in China obeys the emperor.
- why the emperor orders a search to be made for the nightingale.
- who leads the courtiers to the nightingale.

In China, as you know, the emperor is Chinese, and so are his court and all his people. This story happened a long, long time ago; and that is just the reason why you should hear it now, before it is forgotten. The emperor's palace was the most beautiful in the whole world. It was made of porcelain and had been most costly to build. It was so fragile that you had to be careful not to touch anything and that can be difficult. The gardens were filled with the loveliest flowers; the most beautiful of them had little silver bells that tinkled so you wouldn't pass by without noticing them.

Everything in the emperor's garden was most cunningly arranged. The gardens were so large that even the head gardener did not know exactly how big they were. If you kept walking you finally came to the most beautiful forest, with tall trees that mirrored themselves in deep lakes. The forest stretched all the way to the sea, which was blue and so deep that even large boats could sail so close to the shore that they were shaded by the trees. Here lived a nightingale who sang so sweetly that even the fisherman, who came every night to set his nets, would stop to rest when he heard it, and say: 'Blessed God, how

COMMENTARY
The wealthy emperor of China lives in tremendous luxury. His magnificent palace and gardens are famed throughout the world. In the emperor's forest is a nightingale who sings beautifully.

porcelain: fine china
cunningly: cleverly and artistically
mirrored themselves: were reflected

beautifully it sings!' But he couldn't listen too long, for he had work to do, and soon he would forget the bird. Yet the next night when he heard it again, he would repeat what he had said the night before: 'Blessed God, how beautifully it sings!'

From all over the world travellers came to the emperor's city to admire his palace and gardens; but when they heard the nightingale sing, they all declared that it was the loveliest of all. When they returned to their own countries, they would write long and learned books about the city, the palace, and the garden; but they didn't forget the nightingale. No, that was always mentioned in the very first chapter. Those who could write poetry wrote long odes about the nightingale who lived in the forest, on the shores of the deep blue sea.

These books were read the whole world over; and finally one was also sent to the emperor. He sat down in his golden chair and started to read it. Every once in a while he would nod his head because it pleased him to read how his own city and his own palace and gardens were praised; but then he came to the sentence: 'But the song of the nightingale is the loveliest of all.'

'What!' said the emperor. 'The nightingale? I don't know it, I have never heard of it; and yet it lives not only in my empire but in my very garden. That it the sort of thing one can only find out by reading books.'

He called his chief courtier, who was so very noble that if anyone a rank lower than his own either talked to him, or dared ask him a question, he only answered, 'P.' And that didn't mean anything at all.

'There is a strange and famous bird called the nightingale,' began the emperor. 'It is thought to be the most marvellous thing in my empire. Why have I never heard of it?'

'I have never heard of it,' answered the courtier. 'It has never been presented at court.'

'I want it to come this evening and sing for me,' demanded the emperor. 'The whole world knows of it but I do not.'

declared: said with strong feeling
odes: poems of praise
chief courtier: attendant of the highest rank
presented at court: officially introduced to the emperor

COMMENTARY
The nightingale is highly praised in books about the city. This makes the emperor annoyed that he has never heard of it. He insists that it is found and brought at once to his palace to sing for him.

'I have never heard it mentioned before,' said the courtier, and bowed. 'But I shall search for it and find it.'

But that was more easily said than done. The courtier ran all through the palace, up the stairs and down the stairs, and through the long corridors, but none of the people whom he asked had ever heard of the nightingale. He returned to the emperor and declared that the whole story was nothing but a fable, invented by those people who had written the books. 'Your Imperial Majesty should not believe everything that is written. A discovery is one thing and artistic imagination something quite different; it is fiction.'

'The book I have just read,' replied the emperor, 'was sent to me by the great Emperor of Japan; and therefore, every word in it must be the truth. I want to hear the nightingale! And that tonight! If it does not come, then the whole court shall have their stomachs thumped, and that right after they have eaten.'

'*Tsing-pe!*' said the courtier. He ran again up and down the stairs and through the corridors; and half the court ran with him, because they didn't want their stomachs thumped. Everywhere they asked about the nightingale that the whole world knew about, and yet no one at the court had heard of.

At last they came to the kitchen, where a poor little girl worked, scrubbing the pots and pans. 'Oh, I know the nightingale,' she said, 'I know it well, it sings so beautifully. Every evening I am allowed to bring some leftovers to my poor sick mother who lives down by the sea. Now it is far away, and as I return I often rest in the forest and listen to the nightingale. I get tears in my eyes from it, as though my mother were kissing me.'

'Little kitchenmaid,' said the courtier, 'I will arrange for a permanent position in the kitchen for you, and permission to see the emperor eat, if you will take us to the nightingale; it is summoned to court tonight.'

Half the court went to the forest to find the nightingale. As they were walking along a cow began to bellow.

'Oh!' shouted all the courtiers. 'There it is. What a marvellously powerful voice the little animal has; we have heard it before.'

COMMENTARY
Neither the chief courtier nor other officials at the court know where to find the nightingale. The emperor, now furious, threatens to punish them if they fail to bring it to him. Finally, a kitchen servant is found who says she knows where it lives.

fable: an untrue story
artistic imagination: the make-believe of writers
Tsing-pe!: an exclamation in Chinese
permanent position: full-time job
summoned: commanded to come
bellow: moo

'That is only a cow,' said the little kitchenmaid. 'We are still far from where the nightingale lives.'

They passed a little pond; the frogs were croaking.

'Lovely,' sighed the Chinese imperial dean. 'I can hear her, she sounds like little church bells ringing.'

'No, that is only the frogs,' said the little kitchenmaid, 'but any time now we may hear it.'

Just then the nightingale began singing.

'There it is!' said the little girl. 'Listen. Listen. It is up there on that branch.' And she pointed to a little grey bird sitting amid the greenery.

'Is that possible!' exclaimed the chief courtier. 'I had not imagined it would look like that. It looks so common! I think it has lost its colour from shyness and out of embarrassment at seeing so many noble people at one time.'

'Little nightingale,' called the kitchenmaid, 'our emperor wants you to sing for him.'

'With pleasure,' replied the nightingale, and sang as beautifully as he could.

'It sounds like little glass bells,' sighed the chief courtier. 'Look at its little throat, how it throbs. It is strange that we have never heard of it before; it will be a great success at court.'

'Shall I sing another song for the emperor?' asked the nightingale, who thought the emperor was there.

'Most excellent little nightingale,' began the chief courtier, 'I have the pleasure to invite you to attend the court tonight, where his Imperial Majesty, the Emperor of China, wishes you to enchant him with your most charming art.'

'It sounds best in the green woods,' said the nightingale; but when he heard that the emperor insisted, he followed them readily back to the palace.

PAUSE FOR PLAYBACK:
Now look at the playback questions on page 91 before going on with your reading.

COMMENTARY
Sure of her way, the kitchenmaid leads the courtiers to the nightingale in the heart of the forest. The chief courtier is amazed that such a plain-looking bird can sing so sweetly. Other courtiers show their ignorance of nature by mistaking a cow's moo and a frog's croak for the nightingale's song.

Rather reluctantly, the nightingale agrees to sing for the emperor at his palace.

imperial dean: head of the church in China

Look out for…
- **how the emperor feels when he hears the nightingale sing.**
- **what the emperor gets as a present from the emperor of Japan.**
- **what happens to the nightingale after the emperor's present arrives – and why.**

There every room had been polished and thousands of little golden lamps reflected themselves in the shiny porcelain walls and floors. In the corridors stood all the most beautiful flowers, the ones with silver bells on them; and there was such a draught from all the servants running in and out, and opening and closing doors, that all the bells were tinkling and you couldn't hear what anyone said.

In the grand banquet hall, where the emperor's throne stood, a little golden perch had been hung for the nightingale to sit on. The whole court was there and the little kitchenmaid, who now had the title of Imperial Kitchenmaid, was allowed to stand behind one of the doors and listen. Everyone was dressed in their finest clothes and they all were looking at the little grey bird, towards which the emperor nodded very kindly.

The nightingale's song was so sweet that tears came into the emperor's eyes; and when they ran down his cheeks, the little nightingale sang even more beautifully than it had before. His song spoke to one's heart, and the emperor was so pleased that he ordered his golden slipper to be hung around the little bird's neck. There was no higher honour. But the nightingale thanked him and said that he had been honoured enough already.

'I have seen tears in the eyes of an emperor, and that is a great enough treasure for me. There is a strange power in an emperor's tears and God knows that is reward enough.' Then he sang yet another song.

'That was the most charming and elegant song we have ever heard,' said all

COMMENTARY
The palace has been made to look magnificent in the Nightingale's honour. The nightingale sings. Everyone is enchanted, especially the emperor. He is moved to tears and offers the bird a rich reward.

banquet hall: great dining hall
Imperial Kitchenmaid: chief kitchenmaid to the emperor
spoke to one's heart: touched people's deepest feelings

the ladies of the court. And from that time onward they filled their mouths with water, so they could made a clucking noise, whenever anyone spoke to them, because they thought that then they sounded like the nightingale. Even the chambermaids and the lackeys were satisfied; and that really meant something, for servants are the most difficult to please. Yes, the nightingale was a success.

He was to have his own cage at court, and permission to take a walk twice a day and once during the night. Twelve servants were to accompany him; each held on tightly to a silk ribbon that was attached to the poor bird's legs. There wasn't any pleasure in such an outing.

The whole town talked about the marvellous bird. Whenever two people met in the street they would sigh; one would say, 'night,' and the other 'gale'; and then they would understand each other perfectly. Twelve delicatessen shop owners named their children 'Nightingale,' but not one of them could sing.

One day a package arrived for the emperor; on it was written 'Nightingale.'

'It is probably another book about our famous bird,' said the emperor. But he was wrong; it was a mechanical nightingale. It lay in a little box and was supposed to look like the real one, though it was made of silver and gold and studded with sapphires, diamonds, and rubies. When you wound it up, it could sing one of the songs the real nightingale sang; and while it performed its little silver tail would go up and down. Around its neck hung a ribbon on which was written: 'The Emperor of Japan's nightingale is inferior to the Emperor of China's.'

'It is beautiful!' exclaimed the whole court. And the messenger who had brought it had the title of Supreme Imperial Nightingale Deliverer bestowed upon him at once.

'They ought to sing together, it will be a duet,' said everyone, and they did. But that didn't work out well at all; for the real bird sang in his own manner and the mechanical one had a cylinder inside its chest instead of a heart. 'It is not its fault,' said the imperial music master. 'It keeps perfect time, it

---

lackeys: the lowest ranking servants
delicatessen shop: a shop selling expensive
    cooked meats, cheeses, etc.
inferior: of poorer quality
bestowed upon: awarded to

COMMENTARY
Soon the nightingale is made to leave the forest and live at the emperor's court.

One day a present arrives for the emperor. It is a clockwork nightingale made out of precious metals. When wound up, it sings the same song over and over again. The real nightingale is made to sing a duet with the mechanical one. It sounds dreadful.

belongs to my school of music.' Then the mechanical nightingale had to sing solo. Everyone agreed that its song was just as beautiful as the real nightingale's; and besides, the artificial bird was much pleasanter to look at, with its sapphires, rubies, and diamonds that glittered like bracelets and brooches.

The mechanical nightingale sang its song thirty-three times and did not grow tired. The court would have liked to hear it the thirty-fourth time, but the emperor thought that the real nightingale ought to sing now. But where was it? Nobody had noticed that he had flown out through an open window, to his beloved green forest.

'What is the meaning of this!' said the emperor angrily, and the whole court blamed the nightingale and called him an ungrateful creature.

'But the best bird remains,' they said, and the mechanical bird sang its song once more. It was the same song, for it knew no other; but it was very intricate, so the courtiers didn't know it by heart yet. The imperial music master praised the bird and declared that it was better than the real nightingale, not only on the outside where the diamonds were, but also inside.

'Your Imperial Majesty and gentlemen: you understand that the real nightingale cannot be depended upon. One never knows what he will sing; whereas, in the mechanical bird, everything is determined. There is one song and no other! One can explain everything. We can open it up to examine and appreciate how human thought has fashioned the wheels and the cylinder, and put them where they are, to turn just as they should.'

'Precisely what I was thinking!' said the whole court in a chorus. And the imperial music master was given permission to show the new nightingale to the people on the following Sunday.

The emperor thought that they, too, should hear the bird. They did and they were as delighted as if they had got drunk on too much tea. It was all very Chinese. They pointed with their licking fingers toward heaven, nodded, and said: 'Oh!'

But the poor fisherman, who had heard the real nightingale, mumbled, 'It

COMMENTARY
Before long, the real nightingale is found to have flown back to its home in the forest.

The imperial music master claims that the mechanical nightingale sings better than the real one. He says it can always be relied on, though it sings only one song. Everyone at court agrees.

school: style
by heart: note for note
everything is determined: how and what it sings is pre-planned
fashioned: produced, invented

sounds beautiful and like the bird's song, but something is missing, though I don't know what it is.'

The real nightingale was banished from the empire.

The mechanical bird was given a silk pillow to rest upon, close to the emperor's bed; and all the presents it had received were piled around it. Among them were both gold and precious stones. Its title was Supreme Imperial Night-table singer and its rank was Number One to the Left. The emperor thought the left side was more distinguished because that is the side where the heart is, even in an emperor.

The imperial music master wrote a work in twenty-five volumes about the mechanical nightingale. It was not only long and learned but filled with the most difficult Chinese words, so everyone bought it and said they had read and understood it, for otherwise they would have been considered stupid and had to have their stomachs poked.

A whole year went by. The emperor, the court, and all the Chinese in China knew every note of the supreme imperial night-table singer's song by heart; but that was the very reason why they liked it so much: they could sing it themselves, and they did. The street urchins sang: 'Zi-zi-zizzi, cluck-cluck-cluck-cluck.' And so did the emperor. Oh, it was delightful!

But one evening, when the bird was singing its very best and the emperor was lying in bed listening to it, something said: 'Clang,' inside it. It was broken! All the wheels whirred around and then the bird was still.

The emperor jumped out of bed and called his physician but he couldn't do anything, so the imperial watchmaker was fetched. With great difficulty he repaired the bird, but he declared that the cylinders were worn and new ones could not be fitted. The bird would have to be spared; it could not be played so often.

It was a catastrophe. Only once a year was the mechanical bird allowed to sing, and then it had difficulty finishing its song. But the imperial music master made a speech wherein he explained, using the most difficult words, that the bird was as good as ever; and then it was.

---

street urchins: poor children dressed in
    rags
physician: doctor
spared: made to sing less often

COMMENTARY
The emperor banishes the real nightingale from China altogether. A year passes. The real nightingale is forgotten but the mechanical one becomes famous throughout China. One day, however, its clockwork mechanism breaks. To everyone's horror, it is beyond repair.

PAUSE FOR PLAYBACK:
Now look at the playback questions on page 91 before going on with your reading.

Look out for...
- **what happens when the emperor is visited by Death.**
- **how the real nightingale comes to the emperor's aid.**

Five years passed and a great misfortune happened. Although everyone loved the old emperor, he had fallen ill; and they all agreed that he would not get well again. It was said that a new emperor had already been chosen; and when people in the street asked the chief courtier how the emperor was, he would shake his head and say: 'P.'

Pale and cold, the emperor lay in his golden bed. The whole court believed him to be already dead and they were busy visiting and paying their respects to the new emperor. The lackeys were all out in the street gossiping, and the chambermaids were drinking coffee. All the floors in the whole palace were covered with black carpets so that no one's steps would disturb the dying emperor; and that's why it was as quiet as quiet could be in the whole palace.

But the emperor was not dead yet. Pale and motionless he lay in his great golden bed; the long velvet drapes were drawn, and the golden tassels moved slowly in the wind, for one of the windows was open. The moon shone down upon the emperor, and its light reflected in the diamonds of the mechanical bird.

The emperor could hardly breathe; he felt as though someone were sitting on his chest. He opened his eyes. Death was sitting there. He was wearing the

drapes: curtains

COMMENTARY
Five more years pass. The emperor falls seriously ill; no one expects him to get better.

emperor's golden crown and held his gold sabre in one hand and his imperial banner in the other. From the folds of the curtains that hung around his bed, strange faces looked down at the emperor. Some of them were frighteningly ugly, and others mild and kind. They were the evil and good deeds that the emperor had done. Now, while Death was sitting on his heart, they were looking down at him.

'Do you remember?' whispered first one and then another. And they told him things that made the cold sweat of fear appear on his forehead.

'No, no, I don't remember! It is not true!' shouted the emperor. 'Music music, play the great Chinese gong,' he begged, 'so that I will not be able to hear what they are saying.'

But the faces kept talking and Death, like a real Chinese, nodded his head to every word that was said.

'Little golden nightingale, sing!' demanded the emperor. 'I have given you gold and precious jewels and with my own hands have I hung my golden slipper around your neck. Sing! Please sing!'

But the mechanical nightingale stood as still as ever, for there was no one to wind it up; and then, it couldn't sing.

Death kept staring at the emperor out of the empty sockets in his skull; and the palace was still, so terrifyingly still.

All at once the most beautiful song broke the silence. It was the nightingale, who had heard of the emperor's illness and torment. He sat on a branch outside his window and sang to bring him comfort and hope. As he sang, the faces in the folds of the curtains faded and the blood pulsed with greater force through the emperor's weak body. Death himself listened and said, 'Please, little nightingale, sing on!'

'Will you give me the golden sabre? Will you give me the imperial banner? Will you give me the golden crown?'

Death gave each of his trophies for a song; and then the nightingale sang about the quiet churchyard, where white roses grow, where fragrant elderberry trees are, and where the grass is green from the tears of those who come to

COMMENTARY

The emperor is haunted by Death, who shows him ghostly faces representing the good and bad deeds he has done during his life.

The emperor commands the mechanical nightingale to sing; he is trying to drown out the ghostly voices of Death. But, being broken, it remains silent. Suddenly the song of the real nightingale is heard outside the window. Its song is so sweet that it drives Death away.

sabre: the emperor's sword of state
torment: mental suffering, distress

trophies: objects kept as a reminder of success
fragrant: sweet-smelling

mourn. Death longed so much for his garden that he flew out of the window, like a white cold mist.

'Thank you, thank you,' whispered the emperor, 'you heavenly little bird, I remember you. You have I banished from my empire and yet you came to sing for me; and when you sang the evil phantoms that taunted me disappeared, and Death himself left my heart. How shall I reward you?'

'You have rewarded me already,' said the nightingale. 'I shall never forget that, the first time I sang for you, you gave me the tears from your eyes; and to a poet's heart, those are jewels. But sleep so you can become well and strong; I shall sing for you.'

The little grey bird sang; and the emperor slept, so blessedly, so peacefully.

The sun was shining in through the window when he woke; he did not feel ill any more. None of his servants had come, for they thought that he was already dead; but the nightingale was still there and he was singing.

'You must come always,' declared the emperor. 'I shall only ask you to sing when you want to. And the mechanical bird I shall break into a thousand pieces.'

'Don't do that,' replied the nightingale. 'The mechanical bird sang as well as it could, keep it. I can't build my nest in the palace; let me come to visit you when I want to, and I shall sit on the branch outside your window and sing for you. And my song shall make you happy and make you thoughtful. I shall sing not only of those who are happy but also of those who suffer. I shall sing of the good and of the evil that happen around you, and yet are hidden from you. For a little songbird flies far. I visit the poor fishermen's cottages and the peasant's hut, far away from your palace and your court. I love your heart more than your crown, and yet I feel that the crown has a fragrance of something holy about it. I will come! I will sing for you! Only one thing must you promise me.'

'I will promise you anything,' said the emperor, who had dressed himself in his imperial clothes and was holding his golden sabre and pressing it against his heart.

COMMENTARY

Thanks to the real nightingale, the emperor recovers. Having been so close to death, he wants to give the bird a reward. But the nightingale says it is reward enough to have had his singing appreciated for itself. He agrees to sing to the emperor in the future, telling him what happens in the real world beyond the palace.

phantoms: ghosts
taunted: mocked, sneered at

'I beg of you never tell anyone that you have a little bird that tells you everything, for then you will fare even better.' And with those words the nightingale flew away.

The servants entered the room to look at their dead master. There they stood gaping when the emperor said: 'Good morning.'

COMMENTARY

The emperor promises the nightingale never to tell how he knows about what happens in the outside world. His servants arrive. They are astonished to see him perfectly well again.

fare even better: be more happy and wise

Study guide

PLAYBACK QUESTIONS

PAGES 79 to 82:

➤ Look back to the first paragraph. What is unusual about (i) the material out of which the emperor's palace is built, and (ii) the 'most beautiful' flowers in the emperor's garden?

➤ Why does the emperor become so annoyed? What does this tell you about his character?

➤ Why does the humble kitchenmaid know all about the nightingale while the high-ranking courtiers know nothing?

➤ The nightingale says that his song 'sounds best in the green woods'. Do you think he is likely to be right? Why?

Now return to reading the story on page 83

PAGES 83 to 87:

➤ After singing to the emperor, the real nightingale refuses the reward he is offered. What is this reward? What reason does the nightingale give for refusing it?

➤ When the mechanical nightingale arrives, it has a ribbon round its neck. What message is written on it? What do you think is the true meaning of the message?

➤ If you had been the emperor, which of the two nightingales would *you* have preferred to keep? Why?

➤ 'Only once a year was the mechanical bird allowed to sing, and then it had difficulty finishing its song.' Why has this situation come about?

Now return to reading the story on page 87

REVIEWING THE WHOLE STORY: SUGGESTED ACTIVITIES

1 Poking fun

In *The Nightingale*, Hans Andersen makes fun of – or *ridicules* – a number of different people.

a   **In a group**, talk about how the following are made to look foolish at certain points in the story. Take each in turn:

- The Chinese emperor;

- The chief courtier;

- The imperial music master;

- Other members of the emperor's court, including the ladies;

- The townspeople.

b   **In the same group**, discuss why the kitchenmaid and the fisherman are the only two people in the story who do *not* seem foolish. What do these two characters have in common?

c   **As a class**, discuss *why* the emperor and almost everyone around him seem ridiculous. What points do you think the writer is making by poking fun at them or 'sending them up'?

d   **By yourself**, write an account of the way in which Hans Andersen ridicules the emperor and his court. Why does he do so? Use quotations from the story to back up your ideas.

2 Real and artificial birds

Despite its title, this story is really based on *two* nightingales. Make a study of the differences between them.

a   **With a partner**, go through the story noting down briefly all the ways in which the two nightingales are shown to be complete opposites.

b   **By yourself**, draw on your discussion and notes to make a detailed comparison between the real nightingale and the artificial one. Set out your findings in the form of a 'comparison chart', like that shown on the next page.

The real nightingale	The artificial nightingale
Sings because it is in his nature to do so	Sings because it has been 'programmed' to do so

b **Re-join your partner**. Compare charts. If necessary, add to or change any points you have made.

c **By yourself**, imagine that you are the Chinese emperor when he received the mechanical nightingale as a gift. You are wiser, though, than he was. Knowing that the gift is useless, you decide to send it back to the emperor of Japan.

Write the polite letter you send with the returned gift. In it you should explain (i) why you are returning it and (ii) why the Japanese emperor was wrong to think it was a valuable present.

3 The emperor's diary

The Chinese emperor keeps a personal diary. In it he records each day's events and expresses his feelings about them.

a **As a class**, talk about what the emperor would be likely to write on:

- The day he receives the book in praise of his own city;

- The day on which the real nightingale first sings to him;

- The day on which he is visited by Death;

- The day on which he recovers his health.

b **By yourself**, write these four extracts from the emperor's diary. In doing so, you should bring out clearly:

- your understanding of the emperor's character in the first two-thirds of the story;

- the way in which he changes after he becomes ill;

- how he comes to appreciate the real nightingale by the end of the story.

4 | Summary sentences

a **In a group**, try to sum up the main moral or 'lesson' of the story in a single sentence.

Here are five possibilities for you to consider:

● Wealth can't buy you health;

● The things of nature are better than things made by man;

● The poor are wiser than the rich;

● People in authority must be obeyed;

● Freedom is worth more than power.

Talk about each of these in turn. In your opinion, how well-suited is each of them to the story? Which do you consider to be the most appropriate, and which the least?

If you feel you can produce a more suitable 'summary sentence', do so. Be prepared to justify it to the class.

b Round off this activity by holding a **class discussion**, in which you say what your group has decided and compare your ideas with those of other groups.

5 | Your own writing

Choose one of the suggested summaries in Activity 4. Use it as a theme for a piece of your own writing. This can take the form of a story, a poem or a playscript.

a **By yourself**, plan and draft your writing. Show it to your teacher for comment.

b Make any changes you feel are necessary. Then write your second draft.

c Whatever form the writing takes, produce your final version on a computer. If you wish, include suitable graphics and/or hand-drawn illustrations.

Overview

The activities in this section ask you to do two things:

1 Talk and/or write about the stories in order to understand more about the way they are told.

   You will be looking at:

   - **Narrative**   The way a story is built up and organised.

   - **Characterisation**   The way the characters are presented to us.

   - **Themes**   The main ideas and issues the author writes about.

2 Make comparisons between some of the stories.

1 Recipe for a fairy tale

The *events* that occur in the stories in this book are very different. However, the stories still have a lot of similarities. There are characters who are very good, and others who are very bad. There are talking animals and birds. There are unexpected 'twists', dangerous situations, surprise endings…and so on.

a   **As a class**, talk about what 'ingredients' Hans Andersen's fairy tales have in common.

b   **With a partner**, compare the stories you have read in this book, concentrating on the events and the characters. Make a separate column for each story. In each column, list the main characters and the most important things that happen to them, without going into too much detail.

When you have finished, look closely at the items in your columns. How many of them are *common* to each of the stories you have read?

c   **By yourself**, use up to *ten* of these items to write a recipe for a fairy tale. Model the layout and the language on the recipe shown below. Don't forget to add the method of mixing and making your fairy tale, as well as giving the ingredients. If you wish, add small drawings of the ingredients to make your recipe look more attractive.

PLAIN LOAF

$1\frac{1}{2}$ *lb flour*
3 teaspoons salt
$\frac{1}{2}$ *oz yeast*
1 teaspoon sugar
$\frac{3}{4}$ *pint warm water*

Sieve flour and salt into a warm basin. Cream yeast with sugar and add the warm water. Make a well in the flour, pour in the liquid, sprinkle over the top a little flour from the sides. Mix, knead, allow to rise in a warm place for an hour. Shape into a cottage loaf, put on a floured oven sheet, prove for 15 minutes. Bake for 30–35 minutes in a moderately hot oven.

---

2 | Openings and closings

Read or re-read the first and last paragraphs of all four stories in this book. It doesn't matter how many stories you have read right through.

a **With a partner**, make a note chart about these first and last paragraphs, as in the example below. It describes the opening of *The Nightingale*:

Who?	Where?	When?	What happens?
The Chinese emperor (not named), his courtiers and his subjects	The emperor's palace and its gardens	'A long, long, long time ago' — the distant past	Just 'a story' — no clue yet about the main events

Now make a note chart with the same headings about the opening and closing paragraphs of the story below, *James McGee goes to See*:

Opening paragraph
James McGee was tall, dark and handsome (at least, that's what he told his little sister Kim), but he had never been to the seaside. As he got on the coach with the rest of the team, he tried to look calm and casual, but inside him there was a knot of excitement, and in his head a voice kept bubbling away, 'I'm going to see the sea, I'm going to see the sea!'

[The middle of the story is that James has all sorts of adventures, nearly misses the match, scores the winning goal, and gets back on the coach to go home…]

Closing paragraph
There was a murmur of contented voices adding its own rhythm to the beat of the music on the coach-driver's radio.
'What did you think of the town, then?' asked Badger.
James paused, remembering his first sight of the glittering, glamorous water.
'It was all right, I suppose,' he replied. 'You going down the Club tomorrow?'

b   **With the same partner**, compare your notes on Andersen's stories with those you have made about *James McGee goes to See*. What are the main differences between the two kinds of story?

c   **As a class**, discuss what it is about fairy tales that makes their openings and closings special and different from those of other stories.

3 | On trial

Choose any four characters from the stories in this book who behave in either a foolish or a wicked way. You could choose two from *The Tinderbox* and two from *The Nightingale*; or one from *The Emperor's New Clothes* and three from *The Snow Queen*; or any other combination.

a   **As a class**, hold a trial in which each character is made to answer for his or her actions, before a verdict is reached.

How to work

Divide your class into Group **A** and Group **B**. In the first half of the trial, people in Group **A** are the prosecutors and people in Group **B** the accused. In the second half of the trial, it is the other way round.

When your group is prosecuting, draw up a list of questions to put to the accused. For example:

● Where were you when…?

● Why did you decide to…?

● How do you explain…?

Anyone in the group can ask suitable questions.

When your group is acting as the accused, answer in a way that is meant to prove your innocence (or, at least, that shows you have been judged too harshly). Anyone in your group can answer.

Reach a verdict in whatever way you and your teacher decide is most fair. Discuss a suitable sentence to pass on each character.

b   **By yourself**, write a judgement of any *two* characters' actions, basing what you write on the class trial. Include your own verdict and sentence, together with an explanation for giving them.

4 | Repetitions

Hans Andersen preferred his stories to be read aloud as if they were being 'spoken', like the stories told long before writing and print were invented. In order to make them easier to remember, such stories contained a lot of sentences that were *repeated*: almost exactly the same words were used again and again.

a   **By yourself**, skim-read at least two of the stories in this book. Pick out any sentences which you find being repeated. Note them down. Next to each sentence, jot a few words of your own saying (i) what has just happened in the story, and (ii) what is about to happen next.

b   **Join up with a partner**. Compare your 'repeated sentences' and the notes you have made about them. Can you see any pattern to these repetitions? Do they usually come at the beginning or at the end of an 'episode' in the story?

c   **As a class**, pool your ideas about when the repeated sentences occur. Talk about *why* they are there. Is it, for instance:

 ● to speed the story up?

 ● to sum up what has happened so far?

 ● to underline the 'moral' of the story?

What other reasons can you suggest? Are the reasons always the same from story to story?

d   **By yourself**, write a short story entitled *The Land of Pins and Needles*. When planning, make sure that:

 ● it has a clear beginning and ending;

 ● it contains at least three 'episodes', which *must* start or finish with the same sentence.

As you come to write your repeated sentences, try hard to use them in ways that make your story more effective.

5 | Interviewing the writer

Conduct a role-play session in which Hans Andersen is interviewed about his *intentions* in writing one or more of the stories in this book.

a   **With a partner**, draw up a list of questions you genuinely want to ask the writer about the story(ies) you have read. Since Hans Andersen died well over a hundred years ago, they must be able to be answered by an intelligent reader – yourself, for instance.

The questions you ask will depend on the story(ies) in which you are most interested. Broadly speaking, they may include such things as:

●   why Andersen began – and ended – the story as he did;

●   why he introduced a 'twist' at a certain point in the story;

●   how he tried to build up a mood of suspense (that is, a strong feeling of 'what will happen next?');

●   why he decided to make his characters behave in certain ways;

●   how he set about showing the changes that took place in a character as the story developed;

●   why he chose particular settings (that is, places where the action happens) for the story;

●   what moral or 'lesson' he was trying to bring out through the story;

●   how far he was satisfied, or dissatisfied, with a particular story after he had finished it.

b   **Join up with another pair**. Two of you should act the role of Hans Andersen and answer the others' questions as thoughtfully as possible. In the course of the session, change roles at least once so that everyone has the chance to 'be' the writer.

c   **By yourself**, write a question-and-answer interview with Hans Andersen about one or more of his stories. Base it on the role-play session you have had.